"Who are you and what are you doing here?"

Zara was dressed for seduction, her only covering a drape of gauze. She moistened her lips in a manner as unconscious as it was arousing. "I've told you who I am and why I've come."

"Then why are you so nervous?"

Prince Haidar was a handsome man, she acknowledged. Everything about him spoke of strength and power. This was the man who controlled her future.

"If I'm nervous, it's because of who you are." She whispered the confession.

"You have nothing to fear from me. I don't take unwilling women to my bed. Your services won't be required."

Day Leclaire and her family live in the midst of a maritime forest on a small island off the coast of North Carolina. Despite the yearly storms that batter them and the frequent power outages, they find the beautiful climate, superb fishing and unbeatable seascape more than adequate compensation. One of their first acquisitions upon moving to Hatteras Island was a cat named Fuzzy. He has recently discovered that laps are wonderful places to curl up and nap—and that Day's son really was kidding when he named the hamster Cat Food.

Books by Day Leclaire

HARLEQUIN ROMANCE®
3543—THE NINE-DOLLAR DADDY
3564—SHOTGUN BRIDEGROOM
3575—BRIDEGROOM ON APPROVAL (Fairytale Weddings #1)
3579—LONG-LOST BRIDE (Fairytale Weddings #2)
3591—HER SECRET BODYGUARD
3611—THE BRIDE'S PROPOSITION

Don't miss any of our special offers. Write to us at the following address for information on our newest releases.

Harlequin Reader Service
U.S.: 3010 Walden Ave., P.O. Box 1325, Buffalo, NY 14269
Canadian: P.O. Box 609, Fort Erie, Ont. L2A 5X3

TO MARRY
A SHEIKH
Day Leclaire

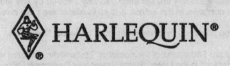

HARLEQUIN®

TORONTO • NEW YORK • LONDON
AMSTERDAM • PARIS • SYDNEY • HAMBURG
STOCKHOLM • ATHENS • TOKYO • MILAN • MADRID
PRAGUE • WARSAW • BUDAPEST • AUCKLAND

To Frank, a Sheikh in civilized clothing.

ISBN 0-373-03623-X

TO MARRY A SHEIKH

First North American Publication 2000.

Copyright © 2000 by Day Totton Smith.

PROLOGUE

Palace of Haidar, Kingdom of Rahman

"ZARA, I'm pleased you have come to visit us." Rasha came forward and held out her hands, her movements graceful despite her advanced pregnancy. "We weren't sure your father would permit it before the wedding."

Zara fought to keep her expression serene. She'd had enough practice at it—a lifetime of practice. "I wasn't certain how welcome I'd be."

"My husband…" Rasha's lips trembled and it took her a moment to firm them. "My husband and I welcome you."

"Thank you." This was impossible. Absolutely impossible. "That's very gracious."

"Hakem would like to meet you now."

"I'm ready," Zara claimed, amazed that she could lie with a straight face.

More than anything, she longed to scream a denial. But that option was forbidden to her. No one denied the request of King Hakem bin Abdul Haidar, especially not a woman in her position. But she wanted to. She wanted to more than anything.

"Your family is well?" Rasha asked, her movements slowed by the child she carried.

"Quite well, thank you. Father and my brothers prosper." Despite years of training in "appropriate" feminine behavior, she couldn't resist adding, "As always."

Rasha offered a brief smile, before sobering. "We were sorry to hear of the death of your mother."

Zara didn't doubt that for a moment. If her mother had lived, this situation would never have arisen. Her mother would have kept her stepfather from such a rash act. But this last year had seen Kadar turn his full focus on advancing his family's political position, without the gentling influence of her mother's compassion and common sense. And Zara was the sacrificial lamb on the altar of Kadar's ambition.

"Thank you. I miss her terribly."

"You'll have to look at us as your family now," Rasha murmured.

Zara didn't know what to say to that, so she remained silent as Rasha led the way through open-air corridors, progressing deeper into the woman's section of the palace. She was a beautiful woman, her features enticingly exotic with light brown eyes and a full, passionate mouth. Her dark hair curled softly over golden shoulders, framing the sort of lush figure Rahman women were renowned for and that Zara would never possess, a realization that had come to her at the great age of twelve. Not that she minded. Except for a few elderly individuals interested in a second or third wife, men had always taken one look at her hair and slender form and rejected her, something even Kadar's substantial influence hadn't been sufficient to change.

Until now.

"Hakem is waiting for us in my quarters. We're in the process of choosing a birthday gift for his cousin. You were probably too young to remember Malik?"

Malik. Zara tried not to react or reveal her alarm. Surely Rasha couldn't mean the Scourge of Rahman? His name had rarely been spoken in her presence and

the few times Zara had heard it, had been in apprehen-
sive whispers far from Kadar's hearing. She'd been
taught from an early age that Malik was an evil, dis-
honorable man, a man intent on destroying Rahman and
bringing ruin to her stepfather and all his children.
Worst of all, he was a murderer. Despite what she'd
been taught, curiosity stirred and she slanted Rasha a
questioning glance.

"He was once in line for the throne, wasn't he?"

"Yes. If he hadn't abdicated, chances are that I'd
have been his wife instead of Hakem's." She shivered,
distress glittering in her eyes. "I can't imagine being
married to anyone else. Not even Malik."

Her comments and reaction confirmed one issue in
Zara's mind. Rasha adored her husband, her love con-
veyed in every look and gesture and word. "Then
you're fortunate he abdicated." A question nagged her.
"But why would your husband send him gifts?"

Rasha's comprehension was instantaneous. "Don't
believe everything you've been told. Hakem and Malik
have a close relationship."

"I thought Malik fled the country."

"He left in order to ensure the peace. But Hakem
often visits the United States to spend time with him."

How odd. Before Zara could ask any further questions, Rasha gestured for her to enter a large sitting
room. King Hakem lounged in a chair, his attention on
a half dozen women standing in a line before him.
Rasha crossed to his side, astonishing Zara by settling
onto the arm of his chair. None of Kadar's wives had
ever been so bold, not even his favorite, Zara's mother.
Hakem's arm immediately went around her, settling on
her extended belly.

"She's here," Rasha murmured.

Hakem glanced her way and Zara knelt as she'd been taught, bowing low and keeping her gaze fixed on the floor. She heard the king leave his chair and approach. "Stand so I may see you," he ordered.

Zara obediently rose. There were so many questions she longed to ask, but a rare show of discretion kept her silent. This was her king and she'd offer the proper respect or suffer Kadar's wrath.

"Remove your veils." He addressed Rasha over his shoulder. "Have you explained to her that it's not necessary to wear them?"

"Her father is very strict."

As soon as Zara had removed the heavy black veil and *abaaya*, he tilted her chin upward, examining her features with a hint of a frown. Compared to Rasha's lush beauty, Zara must seem tame in comparison. Her fine-boned frame lent itself toward a sleek, almost boyish appearance, and her features were pale and delicate, exhibiting none of Rasha's flamboyance.

Hakem lifted a lock of Zara's hair and his frown deepened. Once again she was reminded that the people of Rahman were a superstitious lot. A man interested in marriage avoided a woman with red hair. They were considered shrewish and of questionable morals. And though her hair was more blond than red, she couldn't deny the fiery highlights that streaked through it— flashes of lightning in an otherwise tranquil setting. That touch of red had kept her safe...until now.

"Have you agreed to this marriage?" he asked.

She wished he hadn't asked that particular question. She'd never been good at lying. "My father explained the necessity."

"But is it your desire?"

She fought to recall her mother's training, to remember how she'd used words with the skill of a diplomat. "I have been offered an honor I dare not refuse, Sire," she replied. "I am twenty-two. Unwed. My mother died last year and my family wishes me to find happiness."

"What about your father's people? Your American father, I mean? Have they no desire to meet you?"

She shrugged. "My mother said he had an elderly aunt who attended his funeral. I can't believe she's still alive after all these years."

"And your mother's relatives? What about them?"

"I have a grandmother. She had a falling out with my mother over her marriage to Kadar. Perhaps someday I'll be able to meet her and mend our relationship."

He nodded, his expression still troubled. "What would happen if I decided you weren't acceptable?"

"If you returned me, Kadar would take insult." She could tell by Hakem's grim nod that she hadn't said anything he didn't already know. It would also give her stepfather the excuse he needed to start trouble. For as long as she could remember, he'd plotted and planned for a way to seize the throne of Rahman. "And he's warned that he'll marry me to his uncle."

"The man is seventy, if he's a day," Rasha protested.

Zara smiled matter-of-factly. "I'm not a woman most men would take to wife." She looked directly at Hakem, something she'd been taught never to do. But then, she wasn't the most obedient of daughters and never had been. "Am I?"

"I have no need for a second wife," Hakem said more gently than she deserved. "But if I had, I'd find you quite appealing."

Zara glanced at Rasha, wondering how she'd taken her husband's declaration. Apparently she knew the goodness in his heart and understood that his intentions were well-meant because she nodded in agreement.

"If there were another way out, I'd take it," Zara dared to say. She heard Rasha's soft gasp and ignored it. "Unfortunately I haven't been able to change my stepfather's mind. I assume you haven't met with any better success?"

A stunned silence blanketed the room. An instant later, Hakem laughed in genuine amusement. "Absolutely none, my brazen bride-to-be. Come." He held out his hand. "Since you seem to be a woman of strong opinions, I would have your advice on another matter. One far less crucial to our futures."

He led her to where the six women stood waiting. "I wish to send my cousin a very special thirtieth birthday present. Tell me which one you think he'd appreciate the most."

"You're going to send your cousin a woman?"

"He is a man who has everything." A hint of sadness gleamed in Hakem's pitch-dark eyes. "But perhaps he would enjoy a taste of his homeland."

"And these women? They don't mind being sent to…" She'd already proven herself a brash woman, but for some reason, she couldn't bring herself to speak Malik's name aloud. She shook her head in amused dismay. Perhaps she'd picked up on the superstitions of her adopted people after all. "They don't mind being sent to your cousin?"

"Why would they?" he asked in astonishment. "They have all volunteered for the honor. Malik is a most attractive man."

"She's heard stories," Rasha explained.

"Ah. The stories." His good humor died and Zara shivered in the face of a far different man, one whose anger she wouldn't care to rouse again. "You will not speak of those stories in my presence, Zara. The consequences will be quite severe if you do so. They are lies perpetuated by Kadar and his sons to discredit my cousin and I won't stand for it. Do I make myself clear?"

"Yes, Sire," she murmured.

Could it be true? Were the tales she'd heard all a lie? Did these women actually *want* to go to Malik? She puzzled over the possibility. Everything she'd been told would have suggested they be in terror for their lives. And yet, they stood before her, smiling and contented. Even more telling, anticipation gleamed in their dark eyes and quivered at the corners of their lush mouths. Perhaps Malik wasn't so bad. Certainly her king thought well of him.

An idea came to her then, fully born and complete in almost every detail. A wicked idea. A daring idea. An idea that would thwart Kadar while helping Hakem. A scheme that would give birth to a dream that had haunted her for seventeen long years. All she needed to fulfill her plan was nerve. She studied the six women, one by one, judging which would offer her scheme the greatest chance of success. Finally she stopped in front of the youngest of the women. She was similar in height to Zara and had the most delicate build of the six.

"This one," Zara announced.

Hakem tilted his head to one side. "She is Matana. Her husband died in an unfortunate accident last year, leaving her without family. She would not have been my first choice, which makes me curious. Explain why you have chosen her."

Zara smiled for the first time, a grin that must have caught the king off guard. He stared at her, fascinated, and her spirits lifted. "Because, I believe she'll make the perfect gift. Send her, Sire. I have a good feeling about this. You won't be sorry."

CHAPTER ONE

San Francisco, California

"THANK you for seeing us, Prince Haidar." Two men garbed in traditional Rahman dress hovered in the doorway. "Ali and Jamil, at your service."

Malik Haidar gestured for them to enter his office. "It's a pleasure to welcome you."

Visitors from his homeland were always a treat—if a rare and bittersweet one. The two bowed low, offering him the respect due a man who'd once been heir to the throne, who'd, once upon a time, have been their king. He motioned for them to rise. Years ago, he'd have overreacted to their obeisance, have silently railed at fate's perverse humor. But with age he'd discovered both tolerance, a sense of humor and acceptance of his new life.

"How may I be of service, gentlemen?" he asked.

"We were sent by His Highness," Ali explained. The collar of both his and Jamil's white *thobes* revealed they belonged to the northern part of Rahman, while the gold embroidery decorating the sides of their head scarves indicated the two men were part of the palace staff. "We were given the honor of transporting a gift for your birthday."

Malik smiled, acute pleasure easing the pain of memories long past. His cousin, Hakem, had made this a yearly tradition. Every July without fail, a gift would arrive a few days before Malik's birthday, a ten-year tradition. What would it be this year? More books for his library? Another priceless piece of artwork? Jewelry he didn't need or wear?

"The honor is mine," he assured his visitors.

"If you'll give us a moment, we'll bring it in," Jamil offered. No doubt the two were father and son. There was a familial similarity to the hook of their noses and slant of their eyes. "Your gift is a bit on the heavy side."

Heavy? More and more interesting. "Please. Take your time." Malik settled himself behind his desk and phoned through to his secretary. "Hold my calls for the next hour, Alice. And bring coffee for three as soon as my visitors return."

It didn't take long. The two entered Malik's office carrying a loosely rolled carpet, thick and rich and clearly created by master weavers. His pleasure deepened, nostalgia sweeping over him. He'd deliberately removed all connections to his past from his living quarters. But perhaps he'd made a mistake. Such a rug would make a beautiful addition to his home and he had the perfect place to put it—in his library, right in front of his fireplace.

They set their bundle down on the far side of his office and swiftly unrolled it. Malik had expected a thing of beauty and he wasn't disappointed. But the beauty didn't come from the carpet, as he'd expected. It came from the woman wrapped within the luxurious folds. To his amusement, she tumbled out, sprawling at his feet in a tangled heap of arms, legs and diaphanous black cotton. Her pale skin gleamed through the sheer material and her heavy black hair wrapped around her, clinging to the carpet, to her clothing, and to the bit of pale face exposed by her lopsided veil. He frowned, aware of something odd about her appearance, but unable to determine the cause.

She muttered a curse in his native tongue—one involving her escorts' parentage, a number of camels and an act as impossible as it was humorous. While the two men barked a furious reprimand, Malik grinned. No doubt being forced into a stifling carpet and presented like Cleopatra to Caesar sounded more romantic than the reality of the situation.

"...said nothing about being shoved in a rug!" she complained furiously. "I could have suffocated in there."

It took Ali a moment to recover. He regarded the woman with a brief, horrified gaze before turning to Malik. Wringing his hands, he swallowed hard. "Our apologies, Prince Haidar. Clearly this woman won't be satisfactory. Allow us to contact King Haidar and—"

"You will say nothing to Hakem," Malik cut in, "other than to offer my thanks for his generosity."

A loud knock sounded on the door and his secretary, Alice, pushed it open, pausing in the threshold. Her tray of coffee rattled ominously. Under normal circumstances, she was the most impassive of individuals. Not this time. Taking one look at the girl at his feet, her breath escaped in a shocked gasp. Then her stare shifted to fasten on him in outraged disbelief.

He sighed. He'd established an excellent relationship with his secretary during the eight years she'd been with him. She'd been of invaluable assistance, helping in more ways than he could count as he'd struggled to adjust to his adoptive country. It would appear their relationship had just suffered a serious setback.

"My apologies, Alice," he said gently. "I've been presented with an unexpected gift. Why don't you take the coffee through to the conference room. These two gentlemen will accompany you while I straighten this out.''

It didn't take her long to recover. As a widow in her late fifties, no doubt she'd seen her fair share of unusual sights, though he suspected this would rank up in the top one or two. ''Certainly, Mr. Haidar.'' Her gaze returned to his ''birthday present'' and she lifted an iron-gray eyebrow. ''Is there anything else you require?''

''I think what I have here is quite sufficient,'' he retorted dryly.

Her humor was swift to return. ''But within your powers to handle, I don't doubt.''

He inclined his head. ''Your confidence overwhelms me.'' Suppressing a smile, Alice stepped out of his office and Malik turned to his Rahman visitors. ''Please go with my secretary. I'll join you shortly.''

''Sire, if we've done anything to offend—''

He gestured for their silence. ''I'm not offended. I wish to examine my gift in private.''

Instantly reassured, Ali and Jamil exchanged masculine grins of understanding. Bowing low, they trailed Alice from the room. That left only one further problem to handle. Malik folded his arms across his chest and waited for his ''gift'' to make the first move.

Slowly she inched to the end of the carpet farthest from him and tossed her hair from her face. The Bedouin-style veil she'd used to conceal the lower half of her face sagged beneath her chin. She was breathtaking, though clearly not Rahman-born, despite her colorful curse.

''Come,'' he ordered, gesturing for her to approach. Then, in case she didn't speak English, he repeated his command in Rahman.

She stood with a sigh and walked toward him, her bare feet sinking into the thick carpet. Stopping a discreet few feet away, she stared with a direct gaze that sat at odds with her cautious air. They were interesting eyes, he decided, almond shaped and colored a startling green shot with rays of gold.

"You aren't what I expected," she announced, taking the initiative despite an unmistakable nervousness.

"Nor are you." He could see his irony wasn't lost on her. Despite her wariness, a spark of amusement flickered across her face.

"You have no idea."

Her Rahman was flawless. Unlike Ali and Jamil, her accent came from the south, filled with the richness of that region's Bedouin ancestry. Somehow this unusual woman had been carried to him from the heart of the desert, a pale beauty that had blossomed amid the dark heat of his distant, rebellious brothers. Without a doubt, she lived in a section of the country governed by his nemesis, Kadar, and curiosity consumed him. What was her connection to Rahman and why had Hakem sent her, in particular?

At his continued silence, a mixture of apprehension and curiosity slipped across her face, which didn't surprise him. If she came from the south, her attitude toward him would be tainted by tales of the old days. It was all the more interesting that she'd been chosen as his gift. No woman from Kadar's province would willingly offer herself to the Scourge of Rahman.

Which meant, in all probability, she was unwilling.

"Are you all right?" He gestured toward the carpet. "That couldn't have been comfortable for you. Would you care for something to drink?"

"No, thank you. I've survived the experience, only a

little the worse for wear.'' She tugged at her clothing and adjusted her hair. That's when it struck him, an explanation for the ''wrongness'' he'd sensed. She wore a wig, the intense black of the strands unpleasantly stark against her fair complexion. More and more curious. ''I have to admit, I didn't expect to be rolled up like a pastry and left in there to bake. It's a wonder I didn't suffocate.''

''I gather the Cleopatra act wasn't your idea?''

''No.''

He flicked the long strands of synthetic hair. ''What about the wig? Was that forced on you, as well?''

A hint of alarm flickered across her expressive face, answering his question. The wig had been her idea. Apparently she hadn't expected to be caught out so soon. She didn't say anything—no nervous denials or false outrage. Instead she grew perfectly still as she weighed her options. Not that she had many. If she didn't dispose of the hairpiece, he'd do it for her.

Something in his stance must have warned of his intentions. Giving in to the inevitable, she offered a feminine gesture of surrender and ripped off the veil and wig, tossing them aside. To his amazement, red-gold hair tumbled into her face and down her shoulders and back, the brilliant waterfall of sheet-straight hair concealing her as thoroughly as the veil. He heard her mutter another inappropriate word before thrusting the hip-length cascade from her face. With a few practiced flicks, she brought a semblance of order to the unruly tangle.

She folded her arms beneath her breasts and glared. ''It's red,'' she announced with an edge of defiance.

Her bluntness amused him. Hakem had picked an intriguing gift, though Malik hadn't quite decided how to

respond to his cousin's generosity. Ten years spent in
the United States had changed many of his former at-
titudes. He'd always treasured women, but he now appreciated them far more than he had as a boy of twenty,
seeing past the surface attractions to the strong, capable
individuals beneath.

It hadn't taken long to eventually discover and relish
all the wonderful intricacies of women, women he'd
come to realize who were as adept in their abilities as
any man. Perhaps he'd still be married if he'd come to
that realization a bit sooner. But after following him into
exile, his ex-wife had become Americanized far sooner
than he. Once she'd seen all life had to offer, she'd
decided to explore it without the irritation of a husband
to temper her enthusiasm.

That experience, along with other equally illuminating ones, left him with a significant problem. He regarded that problem with frowning intensity. How did
he rationalize his current philosophy with the tempting
gift standing before him? He'd been given a woman
who was his to take as he wished, whenever he wished.
How did he turn down such an irresistible offer?

"You're frowning," she said. Gathering a handful of
hair, she flicked it in his direction. "I gather that means
you disapprove of me. That's why I wore the wig.
Because I knew you'd hate my hair color."

"I don't hate the color," he responded mildly.

"Most men do. They consider it unlucky."

"Then it's fortunate I'm not a superstitious man."

"Fortunate, indeed. I suppose what's unacceptable in
a wife is acceptable in a…" For a split second her poise
deserted her, revealing a heartrending vulnerability. "Is
acceptable in a birthday present."

Once again, Malik felt the keen sense of wrongness.

He studied the woman with greater care. Perhaps the answer to his concerns would be more easily addressed than he'd thought. If she hadn't come of her own free will, he could offer them both a gracious out. "Who are you and why are you here?"

Her apprehension deepened, dimming the bits of gold shimmering in her gaze. "I apologize, My Lord. I am Zara. King Haidar sent me." She dropped gracefully to her knees and bowed. "I'm your birthday present."

"I see I'll have to raise my standards from now on."

She peeked up at him, her nose wrinkling in appealing confusion. "Excuse me?"

"I would have been satisfied with the carpet."

It took her an instant to absorb his words. Then she chuckled, the sound light and delicious, stirring a reaction that caught him off guard. Hakem had chosen well, though why he'd send someone so fair, instead of one of the dark-haired, dark-eyed beauties more typical to their country, baffled Malik. And a redhead, no less, even if the gold color of her hair contained no more than a mere blush of rose.

Despite Zara's intriguing coloring—or perhaps because of it—he found himself attracted. Perhaps she'd been sent because she didn't resemble the women of his homeland. Hakem might have thought that would be one more indignity added to all the rest. Or perhaps she'd been sent because of her rare beauty.

Whatever the reason, he was tempted to indulge in what she so generously offered—assuming it was freely given. Otherwise, she represented a temptation he'd either have to resist or remove to a safe distance. "I'm no longer a prince, Zara." He cupped her elbow and eased her upward. "You don't need to bow or address me as anything other than Malik. Or Mr. Haidar, if you prefer formality.''

"I was instructed to—"

He deliberately switched to English. "I'm changing your instructions."

"That's your prerogative, of course."

Her English was also perfect, flavored by only the faint sweetness of a foreign accent. His curiosity grew. "Who are you?" he asked again. "Why are you here?"

"I told you already. I'm Zara." She wore a variation of an *abaaya,* the gauzy black cotton covering her from neck to ankle. But he'd never seen one quite so sheer. It flashed tantalizing glimpses of creamy skin as it briefly molded to her body before fluttering away. She drifted across the room, her movements beneath the thin layers dancer-graceful and far too enticing. "As I said…I was sent by your cousin."

"For my birthday."

"Exactly."

"My birthday's not for another three days."

She turned to face him, her eyes narrowing. What thoughts were running through her head now? Something in what he'd said had pleased her. "Yes," she said slowly. "We're early. An easily rectified mistake."

"A mistake?" he prompted.

"I tried to explain to my keepers that there wasn't any need for the Cleopatra imitation." She regarded him with a polite, expectant air. "Perhaps it's a common male fantasy?"

"Very common. All my women come wrapped in a carpet."

Her mouth quivered into a smile. "Right."

He nudged her back to the issue of his birthday. "So you weren't supposed to arrive until my birthday?"

She shook her head. "I'm afraid not."

"Which means that for the next three days…?"

"I'm off limits."

She flitted to the far corner of his office, her *abaaya* billowing in the discreet air currents. What did she have under it? Every time she moved, he caught repeated flashes of pale skin gleaming through the blackness. An intriguing thought occurred. Surely she wasn't nude? She paused in front of his bookcase and inspected the volumes. After satisfying her curiosity, she glanced over her shoulder.

"Perhaps I could return on your birthday?" she suggested, her intonation a bit too casual.

His suspicions intensified. "Or perhaps I should call your… What did you call them? Keepers? Perhaps I should have Ali and Jamil return while we discuss Hakem's precise instructions."

She teased him with her laughter again. "Oh, let's not bother them."

"I thought not."

"Is there a problem waiting to—" he could see her search for a tactful description "—to celebrate your birthday? Ali has my passport, so I'm not going anywhere."

Interesting. "Do you *want* to go somewhere?"

She turned at that. "Oh, yes." An eager smile burst across her face. "I want to go *everywhere*. I want to see everything."

His brows drew together. "Is that why you agreed to come here?" Or perhaps it was how she'd been enticed to do this. Had he been sent a willing participant or a woman plagued by second thoughts? It bothered him that she might have been coerced into this scheme. "Did you agree to be my gift so you could indulge your curiosity for travel?"

"Oh, no. That's just a bonus."

"Which part? Coming here or being my gift?"

He could see the debate raging across her transparent face, her struggle between truthfulness and tact. "Since I'd never met you, I'd have to say that coming here was the bonus."

"Would you like me to help change your mind about that?"

It was the sort of banter he'd have indulged in with any woman. But the minute he spoke the words, the atmosphere in the room became charged with dangerous undercurrents. Before he'd found her amusing, lovely, graceful. Now he found her provocative, filled with an irresistible allure that called to the most elemental part of him. He closed the distance between them surprising a glance of sheer panic from Zara. It stopped him dead in his tracks.

"This is the last time I'll ask." His voice dropped to a warning softness. "Who are you and what are you doing here?"

She took a hasty step backward, pausing in a shaft of sunlight that burned through her clothing. The rapid give and take of her breath stirred the black gauze draped across her breasts, and standing this close, he could see that only a layer or two of sheer cotton preserved her modesty. It answered as many questions as it provoked. She was dressed for seduction, her only covering a drape of gauze. All he had to do was reach out and take what was so blatantly offered. And yet, there was also a refreshing innocence about her that stayed his hand. Instead he studied her, trying to see through her womanly disguises to the truth.

Her makeup was light and emphasized full, kissable lips. Aside from a touch of blush tinting her cheeks, her skin remained free of foundation or powers. She remained caught within the shaft of sunlight, the pure light merciless in revealing flaws. Not that he could find any. Not a freckle marred her skin, which was unusual in a woman so fair, only a tiny pinprick-size mole accenting the sweep of her jaw. But it was her eyes that held him. They dominated her face, every passing thought and emotion revealed in those clear green-gold depths. Right now they warned of her fear—a fear brought on by his questions.

His sense of wrongness intensified.

"Answer my question," he demanded roughly.

She moistened her lips in a manner as unconscious as it was arousing. "I've told you who I am and why I've come."

"Then why are you so nervous?"

Zara shut her eyes for an instant. Fighting for control, she forced herself to return his demanding look, more intimidated by this man than any she'd met before—even her stepfather, Kadar. Malik Haidar was a murderer. An outlaw. And she was all alone with him. From the moment she'd been tossed at his feet, she'd become his to treat as he wished, to do with as he desired, to take and discard whenever the mood struck him.

What a fool she'd been to assume such a risk. Malik continued to hold her with his black gaze, staring as though he could see straight into her soul, his imperious stance demanding answers she didn't dare give. Fear and anguish battled against the tiny bit of determination that still burned within. If only she'd never heard the stories. If only she didn't know him to be a man without honor or compassion. If only she weren't so vulnerable. Because if she'd met him for the first time without the stories haunting her memories, she'd have found him all too appealing.

He was a handsome man, she reluctantly acknowledged, even better looking than King Hakem. Everything about him spoke of strength and power, from his height to his proud posture and bearing, to the intelligence glittering in his eyes. Even dressed in a business suit he exuded a majestic presence she couldn't ignore. This was the man who controlled her future, controlled what would transpire between them over the next few days.

His jaw clenched, warning that his patience would soon run out. She forced herself to battle her fear and focus on what she found attractive about him. Perhaps that would get her through the rest of the interview. In the meantime, she'd offer what honesty she could, since she'd never succeed at lying to this man, at least not when asked such a direct question.

"If I'm nervous, it's because of who you are," she whispered the confession.

She caught the flash of pain that surged through Malik and he actually flinched. "You have nothing to fear from me." He turned his back on her. "I don't take unwilling women to my bed."

This was either really good news or really bad. If only she could discover which. "What are you saying?"

"I'm saying that I find the carpet a more than adequate birthday gift." He turned to face her. Every scrap of emotion had been wiped from his face, harsh lines carving deep grooves on either side of his mouth. Even worse, his eyes reflected a remote coldness that shook her to the core. She hadn't realized how much warmth he'd offered until it had been taken from her. "Your services won't be required."

"You're going to return me?"

Her panic increased. If he sent her back untouched, chances were she'd be in the same desperate straits as when she'd come up with this crazy plan. Knowing her stepfather, her situation could actually worsen. Her only hope was to carry through with her plan and pray Kadar disowned her. Otherwise, Ali and Jamil would drag her home in disgrace. Hakem could honorably refuse to take her for his bride, which would salvage something positive from the ordeal, but she'd still be forced to marry. Only this time it would be to one of the horrid old men who'd been offering for her since her sixteenth birthday.

"Please don't return me to Hakem."

"Why did my cousin choose you of all women?" Malik demanded. "He wouldn't have sent me an unwilling or inexperienced woman. You must have known what you were doing when you agreed to come here."

"I knew."

She needed to get him to stop asking such pointed questions. She couldn't lie about who she was or how she'd reached the decision she had. Not to Malik Haidar. Still, the tales of his infamy were too vivid for total trust. She'd listened well to those cautionary stories. If this man ever learned her identity, he'd manipulate the situation to his advantage if he could. Or perhaps he'd decide to extract a bit of revenge for her stepfather's part in taking away his throne—a revenge that would fall on her all-too convenient head. He'd have another tool for revenge against Kadar, and her stepfather would face the loss of yet another member of his family.

There was another consideration, a far more serious one. If she didn't reassure Malik of her desire to remain, convince him to keep her for a few vital days, all the desperate chances she'd taken would be for nothing. She needed to be thoroughly compromised in the eyes of those back home. If Malik was able to assure everyone of her innocence, King Haidar would be forced to accept her as his bride and Kadar's plots and stratagems would have an excellent chance of succeeding. She'd spend her life trapped in a marriage neither she, Hakem nor Rasha wanted. And she'd never have an opportunity to see the land of her birth, a dream she'd carried since childhood.

Taking a deep breath, she approached Malik. Pausing directly in front of him, she fought for calm, fought to bank the fear, fought harder still to follow the path she'd chosen days ago. Even with her decision made, her heart rebelled. She'd had such dreams of romance and true love. Foolish dreams. Youthful dreams. Dreams that wouldn't have come to pass whether she'd come here or remained in Rahman. She braved herself to stare into Malik's hard, black eyes, to forget all the terrible tales she'd been told about this man.

Gently she slipped her hands up the impressive breadth of his chest and shoulders and laced them at the nape of his neck. His hair was longer than convention dictated, the heavy ebony waves caressing her fingers and wrists. He continued to stand stoically before her, neither accepting her embrace nor rejecting it. The fact that he didn't push her away gave her the courage to take the next step.

"I'm not unwilling," she informed him.

His gaze grew watchful. "Nor are you willing. A man can tell the difference, in case you weren't aware."

"Perhaps you haven't taken into consideration that I'm shy."

His mouth curved into a wry smile. "Is that what you call it? I'd have said you were in a flat-out panic."

"I'm nervous," she conceded.

"Now we're getting closer to the truth."

"I'm being as honest as possible, which is difficult given the circumstances. But I thought you'd prefer honesty." She tilted her head to one side, her silky hair spilling across his chest. "Or am I mistaken?"

"You're not mistaken. But it isn't shy reserve or nervousness I see in your eyes any more than it's desire." He trapped her chin in his palm, lifting her face to his. She gasped at the unexpected touch and his mouth compressed. "It's fear I'm seeing."

In one more second, he'd reject her. She had to act. Now. "Does this seem like fear to you?"

She lifted onto tiptoe and tightened her arms around his neck, slipping her lips across his. By some miracle, she must have done something right because his response was instantaneous. His arms came around her, sweeping down the length of her spine to settle on her hips. He pressed her tight against him, his taut thighs colliding with her softer, feminine curves.

"You kiss like an innocent," he murmured.

She didn't quite know how to respond to that, so she spoke from the heart. "Then show me how you want me to kiss."

CHAPTER TWO

MALIK took control of the embrace. His hands tangled in Zara's hair and he urged her closer. His mouth locked with hers, easing her lips apart. She shivered at the first touch of his tongue. To her delight, he didn't attack, but teased, exploring with such gentle care that her earlier fears dissolved.

"That's better," he murmured.

Oh, yes! "Much better."

At her laughing confirmation, he kissed her again. Deeper. Longer. Harder. Backing the few steps to his desk, he settled his hips on the edge and spread his legs, propelling her between them.

It was a deliberate seduction, one she found irresistible. She'd never known a man's touch. Not like this. Not a touch that contained such blatant masculine aggression, aggression held in careful check. Still... That didn't keep her from detecting the scent of hunger blooming between them or the sexual turbulence disrupting the air. The fear she'd experienced at being given to the Scourge of Rahman subsided, replaced by unruly desire. Was this what her stepfather had guarded her against? Was this what she was expected to share with Hakem Haidar if she'd become his wife?

She broke the kiss, shivering. No. She'd spent time with Hakem, had been briefly touched by him. And she hadn't perceived any hint of response, at least not the sort she'd felt from the start with Malik.

"Kiss me, Zara," he ordered. "Show me that you're here because you want to be."

He'd taught her a lot in the few moments she'd spent in his arms, enough to know how she needed to respond. She feathered her hands along his angled cheekbones and into the dark waves of his hair. Tugging his head downward, she caught his lower lip in a playful nip before settling her mouth over his. He allowed her to take control, though she sensed he held back on some level, kept a part of himself in check. Finally, when she'd kissed him as thoroughly as she knew how, she ended the embrace. His warm laughter gusted across her face and she breathed it deep into her lungs. It intoxicated her, joining them in some strange way.

She'd lived in Rahman since she'd been a child of five, and throughout her years there she'd been constantly nagged by the sensation that she didn't quite belong. But here in Malik's arms, that sensation dissipated. Even when his hands trailed from her hip to the upper curve of her buttocks, she didn't panic.

For some reason her submissiveness amused him. Smiling, he wrapped her hair around his fist and pulled her head back, exposing the length of her neck. "You're playing with me, aren't you?" he murmured. His mouth skated from the pulse throbbing beneath her ear to the hollow at the base of her throat. "I like it. It's nice."

Her eyes drifted closed beneath the silky caress. "Playing?"

"Teasing. Tempting. Shying away one minute before allowing me to explore the next. Giving me a taste without letting our passion get too far out of control."

Is that what he thought? She didn't dare correct him. Surely this wasn't simply a prelude. How was it possible, when it felt like so much more? His hand stroked her hip, his fingers splaying across her abdomen, staking a claim with their unexpected invasion. When she didn't protest, he inched downward. It was too much, too soon. She bucked in reaction, driving her hips tighter against his, feeling the unmistakable ridge of his desire.

"Easy, my sweet. Tell me what you want and it's yours."

He didn't give her time to explain or even react to his misunderstanding. His mouth closed over hers once again, hungry and demanding, giving no quarter in his taking. He continued to hold her in place with one hand, the other sliding from her hair to cup her breast, his thumb rubbing the tip into painful excitement through the textured cotton. Pleasure coalesced into a throb of need and she squirmed as much from the desire to more fully explore the sensations he roused as from the panic that urged her to escape before matters went too far.

Tears of confusion pricked her eyes. "Malik, please."

"You're right," he muttered reluctantly. "Any more and we won't be able to stop."

He set her from him, which calmed her fears but did little to satisfy the painful ache his touch had roused. She hadn't anticipated this, the ungovernable emotions running wild and free, surging through her with unbelievable power. If anything, she'd been dreading the few days she'd have to spend with Malik. She'd known from the moment she'd come up with this plan that her time with him would be as inescapable as it was necessary, that in his arms she'd win her freedom and protect her king, while losing some innocent, romantic core that had always been a part of her. Even the knowledge of all she had to gain didn't ease the anguish over what she stood to lose.

Now confusion colored every thought and emotion. Malik wasn't at all what she'd anticipated. At best, she'd expected to fear him. If her fears had proven accurate, she'd planned to walk out the door and disappear into the country of her birth.

But that wasn't what she'd found. Despite the stories she'd been told, she couldn't detect any cruelty in his nature. At least, not yet. There hadn't been any avarice in his dark eyes when he'd gazed at the carpet—or at her. The only expression she'd detected had been a genuine appreciation for the workmanship of the rug and concern for her well-being. Nor had there been selfishness or anger or any other suspect emotion in his demeanor when dealing with his secretary, Alice. Although Zara sensed a core of iron hardness, he hadn't used his innate strength to control those around him.

So far, she'd glimpsed humor and wry acceptance in his dealings with others. He'd handled an awkward situation with diplomacy rather than arrogant disregard. And even his current annoyance stemmed from his suspicions that she was an unwilling participant. If she stayed, he wanted it to be her choice, not a decision forced upon her.

Was it possible that the stories about him weren't true? She shivered, unwilling to risk so much on instinct, rather than hard, cold fact.

He snagged her chin and turned her face to his, interpreting her expression with uncanny accuracy. "You look confused."

"I'm feeling confused," she confessed.

"I gather I'm not what you were expecting. What sort of man did you think you'd find?"

She knew better than to answer that one. There was

a very good reason for her fear, one she couldn't explain—at least, not to him.

Malik's disgrace had come on the heels of losing her natural brother, Jeb, in a car accident. She and her brother had been close. Very close. His death had traumatized Zara and she'd turned for solace to the youngest of her stepbrothers, Paz, who'd been of a similar age. Though he'd been kind, sharing her grief, he'd loved sneaking into her bedroom at night and weaving wicked stories of monsters in the shape of the Scourge of Rahman.

How could she tell Malik that? How could she explain that his name was used to frighten little girls? Zara shook her head. She couldn't.

"I'll tell you what sort of man you're *not* supposed to be." She evaded his question with a touch of humor. "You're not supposed to be able to read my thoughts."

"Then you should learn to conceal them better. I thought all women were taught that at an early age."

He tucked her hair behind her ears as he spoke, the gesture oddly intimate. How strange that she'd accept his touch without a qualm. After all she'd been told about him, she should feel a hint of apprehension, some tincture of fear. But she didn't. The only turbulence disturbing the tenor of her thoughts came from the lingering desire simmering between them. Her body was open to him, soft and compliant and flushed with warmth, while her emotions were a bewildering combination of want—and shock at that wanting.

She forced herself to ignore her confusion and answer his question. "Not all women are taught to conceal their thoughts. My mother preferred honesty over all other qualities." Her comment elicited a pang of regret. Her mother definitely wouldn't have approved of Zara's current activities. She'd have considered them far from honest. "And after that she demanded—"

"Demanded what?"

Zara swallowed, glancing away. "Personal integrity."

"She sounds like an unusual woman."

"She was."

"Was?" Instant comprehension gleamed in his dark eyes, along with a surprising compassion. "I'm sorry. You must miss her."

"I do."

If she were ever to get through the next few days, she had to change the subject. Talking about her loss only reminded her of the values she'd chosen to compromise. Her mother would have been appalled by what Zara planned. Of course, if her mother had lived, the current choices wouldn't have been necessary. Zara took a steadying breath. Time to force the issue.

She eased free of his arms, hoping a bit of distance would allow her to employ logic instead of emotion in determining the course of the next few days. "So, Prince...Mr. Haidar. Do you find me acceptable as a birthday present?"

"More than acceptable." His mouth pulled to one side. "You must know that after the kiss we exchanged."

If she were a different sort of woman, Zara would have used the blush that warmed her cheeks to her advantage. She'd have smiled shyly and peeked up at Malik from beneath her lashes. Or used a honeyed voice to win a favor. She'd seen it done often enough before, though she'd never been terribly impressed by those women. She refused to pretend to be anything other than she was, despite her current deception.

Determined to preserve a modicum of truth in their relationship, she gave him a direct look and inclined her head in agreement. "Your kiss surprised me," she admitted. "But I'd rather not take anything about your future plans for granted."

She'd amused him. At least it was a more acceptable reaction than the one she usually received at home. Her stepfather would sigh in frustrated resignation, while her stepbrothers would portray a more open annoyance and warn that she'd never find a husband if she didn't learn to show some sort of feminine grace. Only her mother would have given her approval and followed it up by expressing her support to both her husband and stepsons in no uncertain manner.

"You're welcome to stay, if that's your wish," Malik said. "Once you agree, I'll settle the matter with Ali and Jamil."

She framed her next question with care. "Could you find out how long we have?" At least she hadn't said, "How long must I stay?"

For some reason she'd amused him again. He closed the distance between them, invading her space. Even as she took a hasty step back, she swayed forward, making it easy for him to gather her up for another lingering kiss. Desire exploded, terrifying in its strength.

"Hasn't this been explained to you?" He openly caressed her through the thin cotton covering she wore, his touch blatantly possessive. She shivered, helpless to control sensations she'd never experienced before. It was too much, too fast. "We have as long as I say."

Oh, dear. This would never do. She'd secretly planned to slip away from Malik and her keepers and find one of her relatives, thereby avoiding giving herself to a man she didn't know. At the very least, she'd anticipated disappearing into this huge, beautiful country and hiding herself for a while. Her goal had been to find a job, while she decided what she wanted to do with her life. If all else failed, she'd expected a night or two of sin before receiving her freedom. But to remain with this man for the next several days...or weeks...or—she swallowed nervously—or *months* definitely wasn't part of her scheme.

He tilted his head to one side, his gaze far too perceptive. "I've frightened you, haven't I?"

She slipped from his grasp, aware of how much she gave away by fleeing, but unable to help herself. "A little."

"Why?"

"I didn't expect you to keep me for an indefinite period of time. I don't know how long you have in mind." Her hands fluttered. "I'd be more comfortable if we could come to a more definite agreement."

"No, I mean, why are you frightened? You claim you agreed to this, and yet..." He shook his head. "Something doesn't feel right."

She stood to lose all the ground she'd gained with that kiss. Still, she couldn't bring herself to lie. She'd never pull it off successfully. "I'm nervous, not frightened. And I'm nervous because I've never been anyone's birthday gift before. I don't quite know what to expect."

"Hakem didn't offer specifics?" His eyes narrowed, fixing on her with nerve-racking intensity. "That's not like him."

Zara struggled to recall the instructions she'd been given by Matana, the girl originally chosen for Malik. "I'm to be polite. Obedient. To give you pleasure." She released a wry laugh. "I'm not doing too well, am I?"

"Have I complained?" He rested his hip on the corner of his desk and gestured for her to continue. "What else were you told?"

Her color intensified. "To give you a memorable birthday."

"Is that it?"

"That's all I recall."

"Nothing was said about how long you were to stay?"

"No, Sire."

"Malik, remember?" His gaze softened. "If we agree to a definite time frame, would that make you feel more secure?"

"Yes, please."

She wished she could read his expression, but he concealed his thoughts with an ease she envied. "You may leave anytime you want. Just say the word and I'll arrange for your return to Rahman. As I've already told you, I don't take unwilling women to my bed."

The idea of having a say in the matter intrigued her. "Are you suggesting we have equal power? Either one of us can end your birthday celebration?"

He inclined his head, a quick grin slashing across his face. "Equal power. Absolutely."

She decided to take a final risk. "I only have one other request."

"Name it."

She fought down the urge to pace the room, though she suspected he'd noticed her agitation, even without that telltale action. He'd already proven himself an observant man and the way her *abaaya* fluttered around her ankles like nervous handkerchiefs dancing in an unseen breeze, unquestionably gave her away.

She shouldn't be fooled by his softness toward her.

She sensed the underlying hardness within him. She also knew if she pushed too far, that hardness would come down on her full force. He'd treated her kindly so far, but all that could change with one wrong word.

"Your birthday's three days away. Could we use those days to become accustomed to each other?"

"Why?"

"I just need a little time to get to know you."

"You had this time with the other men you've slept with?"

How in the world did she get out of this one? She scrambled for an answer. "I've never been intimate with a man I've only known a few short hours."

"Or a few short days, I assume."

"That, too," she conceded with a shrug.

"Very well. If it would make you more comfortable. You may have your few days."

"Thank you."

"I'll speak to Jamil and Ali." He straightened, one minute a sleepy panther, the next an intimidating predator. "I'll also ask Alice to provide you with suitable clothing."

She fell back a step. "I'd appreciate that. I'm feeling a bit underdressed."

He lifted an eyebrow. "Do you have anything on besides your *abaaya?*"

She hadn't thought he'd noticed what she wore or how she looked. There hadn't been anything blatant in his expression or the tone of his voice. Now she saw that he'd simply hidden it beneath an impassive mask. He'd been well aware of how little she wore, had no doubt seen all she'd have preferred to keep hidden. He'd simply salvaged her dignity by pretending not to notice.

"No, I don't have anything else on," she admitted shortly. She cursed herself for cowardice even as she retreated as far from Malik's reach as possible. "This was Jamil's idea. It's extreme, I realize."

"But effective." His dark gaze swept over her, seeming to burn through the black gauze, leaving her painfully vulnerable. Then, like the flick of a light switch, his regard grew impersonal once again. The difference was...now she knew of his awareness and could no longer hide behind the comforting pretense that he hadn't noticed her nudity. "Did they bring anything else for you to wear?"

"Ali and Jamil have my luggage, what there is of it." For some odd reason, tears threatened. How peculiar. "They were being practical, so I don't have much with me."

"Don't worry. I'll take care of it."

If he offered another kind word, she'd break down completely. She hadn't expected to react this way, to feel such an overwhelming array of emotions. In fact, she hadn't expected to feel anything at all, other than a vague distaste for the duty required of her. She took a quick, steadying breath. She didn't dare fall apart in front of him. Without question, tears would see her on the next flight home.

"Wait here for Alice," he instructed. "She'll arrange for whatever you need."

"I don't need much."

For some reason, her hasty comment drew a smile. "In that case, I'll give Alice instructions for what *I* think you need."

"But—"

He didn't allow her to finish. "I wouldn't want you to shortchange yourself. And I suspect if I didn't take care of it, that's what you'd do." He crossed to the office door. "Wait here while I speak to Jamil and Ali."

His tone had acquired that gentle quality again and she didn't know how to respond. He bewildered her, his attitude so different from what she'd expected she couldn't begin to reconcile the two "Maliks" in her mind. Deciding silence would serve better than any comment she could possibly make, she stood quietly at one end of the room and watched him leave. Within a few minutes, his secretary entered the room.

Alice proved as efficient as she was unquestioning. If she found it strange that Malik's "guest," as she referred to Zara, came without clothes, she didn't let on. "Are there any colors you prefer?" she asked, making a quick notation on the list she'd attached to her clipboard.

"I'm not particular."

The secretary shot her an amused glance. "Mr. Haidar warned you'd say that."

Zara sighed. "And how were you instructed to respond if I did?"

"I was to order the clothing he specified."

"Which would be...?"

Alice smiled. "It's a surprise. But I promise you'll like his choices. Mr. Haidar has excellent taste."

"Anything's better than what I'm wearing."

Curiosity radiated from the secretary, but she impressed Zara by refraining from asking questions. "There's a boutique not far from here. I'll request that they messenger the clothes over right away. Mr. Haidar won't be available for an hour or two. He said to make yourself comfortable and feel free to read any of the books or magazines in the office."

Time to test how much freedom Malik would allow.

"Is there somewhere else I could wait?" she asked, praying her casual tone didn't ring false. "Somewhere that won't disrupt Mr. Haidar's business?"

"Oh, he doesn't mind sharing his office. If there's anything you need, I'll be happy to bring it to you."

It was diplomacy at its best. It also confirmed her worst fears. The ever-efficient Alice wouldn't allow Malik's property to slip away. Zara kicked at the hem of her *abaaya*. Not that she'd get far in what she currently wore. "I'm sure I'll be quite comfortable," she murmured.

"Are you hungry? Would you like something to drink, Miss—?"

"It's Zara. Just, Zara. And I appreciate the offer, but I'm not hungry or thirsty."

"In that case, I'll let you know the minute your clothes arrive." The secretary hesitated. "I'll be right outside the door if you need anything more. Anything at all."

Zara nodded, wondering if she looked as woebegone as she felt. Probably, considering the maternal concern she saw filling Alice's gaze. "Thank you. I appreciate all your help."

For the next hour, she measured the length and breadth of the room with her pacing, picking up the occasional book or magazine before returning it, unread. Aside from the endless hours on the plane, she hadn't had much time to consider the ramifications of her impulsive decision to switch places with Matana. The interminable hours flying to the United States had been spent in perpetual fear of having her deception uncovered by Jamil and Ali, despite being fully veiled throughout the trip. She'd even been afraid to sleep, terrified that her veil would slip, revealing the distinctive color of her hair.

Now she had ample opportunity to consider what she'd gotten herself into, and the full consequences of her decision terrified her. If no one discovered what she'd done, there was a very real chance she'd be forced to allow Malik's possession.

Unless she escaped.

The mere thought of all that would entail threatened to overwhelm her. It was too much, considering her growing exhaustion. She glanced toward Malik's couch, the soft cushions calling to her. She'd just shut her eyes for a few minutes, she decided, unable to resist the lure of sleep. Just long enough to regain her strength and consider how she might slip away from Malik and her keepers. Maybe she could also figure out what she'd do for money until she found her mother's relatives. Or how she'd even find them.

Curling up on the couch, she squeezed her eyes shut. Later. She'd worry about all that after she'd slept. Her chin trembled and tears clung to the tips of her lashes.

It wasn't like her problems were going anywhere.

Malik pushed open the door to his office, one swift look alerting him to Zara's absence. Fury at his foolishness for leaving her unattended vied with a hard-hitting concern for her safety. He hadn't realized how fully he'd accepted responsibility for her. Or how possessive he'd begun to feel toward Hakem's gift to him.

He turned, about to confront Alice over Zara's disappearance when he caught a flash of reddish-gold out of the corner of his eyes. He glanced toward the couch, relief easing both his annoyance and his concern. No wonder he hadn't seen her. Her *abaaya* melted into the black cushions of the couch, making her almost invisible. If it hadn't been for her distinctive hair color, he'd have overlooked her altogether.

He silently approached the couch and gazed down at her. He'd been detained longer than anticipated and jet lag had clearly caught up with his guest at some point during the lengthy wait. She'd curled into a ball on her side, her black *abaaya* pulled taut across the womanly curve of her hips and thighs, the material sheer enough for him to see that she was indeed nude beneath the garment. He stooped beside her and fingered a strand of her hair, shaking his head in amazement. The color and texture was like a silken river of flame, flowing around her delicate features before spilling across the dark cushions to the floor. How had such an exquisite beauty come from Rahman when her coloring proclaimed her Western heritage? And what the hell was he to do with her?

Every primitive instinct he possessed urged him to rip away the cotton swathing her and take what had been freely offered. But another, more civilized part warned he should be cautious. He couldn't rid himself of the unsettling feeling of "wrongness," and until he did, he would follow the dictates of his brain and ignore his baser cravings.

A light tap sounded on his office door. "Mr. Haidar?" Alice poked her head into the room. "Zara's clothes have arrived."

"Bring them in. Quietly, please."

The secretary entered his office, clutching the handles of a half-dozen, overstuffed shopping bags. As he helped relieve her of the load, she gestured toward the couch. "Poor thing," she whispered, shaking her head.

"She must be exhausted. Would you like me to find accommodations for her?"

"She'll be staying with me." His response came more harshly than he'd planned, his possessive tone drawing a puzzled glance from his secretary. How could he explain to her what he couldn't explain to himself? For the time being, Zara was his and he wasn't about to let her out of his sight. Even the thought of installing her in a hotel met with a fierce inner resistance. He wanted her in his home, close to his sight and touch and hearing. "Until I determine what to do with her, I intend to keep her safe."

Alice snorted. "If you can call that safe."

He didn't take offense. He'd known his secretary too long for that. "Don't you trust me with her?"

She glanced at the sleeping woman. "I wouldn't trust her with a saint."

"And I'm far from a saint."

Alice neatly sidestepped that one. "What about the gentlemen from Rahman?" she probed delicately. "Aren't they responsible for her?"

"They're returning home now that they've delivered their 'parcel,' as they referred to her."

"So she really is alone."

"No, Alice. She has me."

And that said it all. Zara had been given to him and he was keeping her until she demanded her release. If he had anything to say about it, it would take a long, long time for her to reach that particular decision.

Malik turned to Alice. "I have more work to finish before calling it a day, but you may leave."

She inclined her head. "Very well, Mr. Haidar. Is there anything else I can do for you?"

"No. I'll see you tomorrow morning, as usual."

"Yes, sir."

His secretary left without another word and Malik returned his attention to Zara. She continued to sleep, oblivious to the turmoil she'd stirred, a faint frown lining her brow. It would seem her dreams were far from happy. Why? he couldn't help but wonder. She claimed to be here of her own volition. The kiss they'd exchanged had confirmed that, as well as her attraction to him. So what was wrong? Why did doubts continue to plague him?

Malik shook his head. There would be plenty of time to get to know her, to find the answers to his questions and discover why she'd agreed to come to him. In the meantime, he'd be patient. He crossed to his desk, determined to lose himself in work while he waited for her to wake.

It took two full hours.

The softest of sighs had the unsettling ability to instantly distract him from the intricacies of a spreadsheet. He watched with interest as she rolled over on the couch in a swirl of black gauze and rumpled hair, her bewildered gaze flickering from one side of the room to the other before landing on him.

Recollection lit her hazel eyes. "I fell asleep," she said in a voice rough with exhaustion.

"You've been out quite a while."

"I didn't mean to sleep so long. I only planned to close my eyes for a minute or two."

"No doubt you needed the rest." He shoved back his chair. "Hungry?"

She sat up, tugging her *abaaya* into place. "Starving."

"I've already eaten. But Alice left something for you

in the refrigerator. That should tide you over until we get to my place.''

Unfortunately she reacted as he suspected she would. Her eyes widened and a hint of nervousness wiped away the last of her sleep-fog. He caught the unmistakable glint of fear before she hastily suppressed it. It wasn't the first time he'd seen that particular look and he ground his teeth in frustration. What the *hell* was going on? Why was she frightened of him?

CHAPTER THREE

"YOUR place?" Zara repeated.

Malik lifted an eyebrow. "Problem?" he asked blandly.

"I don't understand." Her nervousness was palpable. "What happened to Ali and Jamil? Won't I be staying with them?"

"That would be a little difficult since they're on their way back to Rahman."

Clearly she hadn't been forewarned of their plans. "They've gone home?"

"Didn't they tell you?"

"They must not have thought it necessary. I assumed they'd stay until we'd—" She moistened her lips. "Until you'd—"

"Until our relationship came to an end?" he inserted smoothly.

"Yes."

"Since we haven't set a definite date when that's to occur, there's no point in their waiting, is there?"

She bit down on her lower lip and shook her head.

"What's wrong, Zara?"

To his frustration, she shook her head again. Whatever was bothering her ran deep, too deep to reveal on such short acquaintance. She wouldn't be coaxed into blurting it out in a moment of unthinking exhaustion. Patience, he reminded himself once more. She deserved patience.

He defused the situation by starting for the door. "I'll

get you something to eat.'' He gestured toward the
shopping bags neatly piled near the couch. ''These are
the clothes Alice arranged for you. Choose something
to wear. I'll give you time to change.''

The instant the door closed behind him, Zara slipped
from the couch and upended the contents of the bags
onto the cushions. She trusted Malik to do as he'd
promised, but she didn't want to take the chance that
he'd walk in at an inopportune moment. The first thing
she searched for were underclothes. Jamil had been adamant about what she'd wear to meet Malik and she'd
been painfully embarrassed at the garment he'd given
her—or rather, the lack of additional garments.

To her frustrated amusement, the virginal white bra
and panties the bags contained didn't offer any more
protection than what she currently had on. The scraps
of silk and lace were beautiful, but as fragile as they
were sheer. Nevertheless, they were something.
Throwing off her *abaaya* she slipped into them. There
were several pairs of slacks, which she tossed aside before coming across a gorgeous calf-length ivory silk
skirt and matching lace blouse that had an almost
Victorian appearance to it.

As soon as she'd dressed, she neatly folded the remaining clothes back into the bags. There were also
toiletries and Zara silently blessed Alice for her fore-
sight. Best of all she found a purse, a brush and a clip
for her hair. It only took a few moments to bring the
unruly strands under control and coil them on top of
her head. Then she resumed her seat on the couch and
contemplated her bare toes until Malik returned.

''Alice did a wonderful job,'' she greeted him. ''But
she forgot one thing.''

He set a covered platter on his desk. "And what's that?"

She wiggled her toes. "Shoes."

"You have no shoes?"

"Not a one."

"You were brought all the way from Rahman barefoot?"

"No, I had sandals." She tilted her head to one side in consideration. "I think Ali put them in my luggage. Did he give you my case before he left?"

"I'm afraid not."

"I guess I'll make do without them." She spared a quick smile. "It could be worse. I could still be rolled up in a carpet dressed in that rather interesting excuse for an *abaaya* Jamil chose."

"Not a woman's fantasy, I gather."

"Not given the circumstances, no."

"And under other circumstances?" There was an intentness in his gaze, which made her feel more exposed than when she'd stood practically naked before him. It was as though he found her an intriguing puzzle to be solved. "Would the *abaaya* have been an enjoyable fantasy if our relationship had been of longer duration?"

She'd have to be careful. Very careful. This wasn't a man easily fooled. She had a part to play if she didn't want him to realize there was something wrong. She'd already raised too many concerns, judging by some of the questions he'd asked so far. If he decided she wasn't who she claimed, she'd find herself in serious trouble. She dreaded to think what he'd do if he uncovered her true identity.

"If we weren't strangers, it might make for an intriguing fantasy," she conceded.

"You mean if we were intimate."

"No, I mean if we knew each other better. Had a..." She floundered briefly. "If we had built the sort of relationship that allowed us to be comfortable with that level of openness."

"You're avoiding the issue."

Anger flared. What did he want her to say? "Am I supposed to like prancing around nude in front of a man I don't know?"

He shrugged. "Isn't that why you've come?"

"*No!*"

She clapped a hand across her mouth, wishing with all her heart she could steal back that one, disastrous word. She'd done precisely what she'd struggled so hard to avoid. In thirty short seconds she'd forgotten the role she was to play and responded instinctively, instead of in character. With that single, desperate "no," she'd made a terrible mistake.

And they both knew it.

"No?" She shivered at the dangerous softness in Malik's voice. He slowly approached. "Explain yourself, Zara. If you're not here for my pleasure, then why were you sent to me?"

Zara lifted her chin in a manner Malik recognized as customary for her. Anytime she felt under attack, that elegantly curved jawline would firm up and she'd fix her gaze on him with a directness he admired.

"I was sent for your enjoyment. But I'm not a woman off the streets."

"Have I suggested you were?" he demanded, insulted. "Have I treated you with anything other than respect?"

"No. You've been very kind." She clasped her fingers together, refusing to back down, even before his anger. "But if you're expecting me to act the part of an easy woman, you'll be disappointed."

"I'm not interested in that sort of woman and I'd be insulted if Hakem sent me one. If you share my bed it will be from choice, not out of duty or financial gain." His words struck hard and she escaped his scrutiny by darting from the couch to the tray he'd left on his desk. She lifted an eyebrow in an unspoken question and he gestured impatiently. "You don't need to ask my permission, Zara. Help yourself."

She removed the cover, her hand hovered between the strawberries and the grapes. "I assume you want more from me than momentary pleasure," she explained.

"I thought we'd already established that."

"I meant, more than just a sexual encounter." She selected a deep red strawberry and bit into it, catching the explosion of juices with her fingertips. "Conversation. Shared ideas. Activities outside the bedroom."

He frowned as he considered her words, deciding to take them at face value. "Intimacy has many levels and I wouldn't mind exploring them all with you."

She seemed to mull that over as she ate. If there had been the least bit of coyness in her expression, he'd have suspected their conversation was a deliberate flirtation. The picture she made of Victorian purity combined with the delicate greed she displayed while consuming the strawberry could have been a calculated attempt on her part at some gentle foreplay. If so, it worked. The juice stained her lips with a ripeness he longed to taste and the clip she'd used to control her hair only stirred the urge to rip it free and watch the waves of fire tumble down her back.

Yes, he wanted far more than momentary pleasure

with this woman. One night wouldn't be enough—the kiss they'd exchanged had proven that. If she required a few days to feel comfortable before joining him in his bed, then he'd give her the time she required. Of course, that didn't mean he wouldn't do his best to seduce her into changing her mind.

"Sit down and eat," he requested. "Relax."

She hesitated for an instant before sinking into the chair behind his desk. The tray was filled with finger food—slices of fruit and raw vegetables, wedges of sandwiches, along with a cup of creamy yogurt.

She started to help herself, hesitating before selecting a sandwich. "Would you like some," she asked politely.

"No, thanks. It's all yours."

When she finally pushed the tray aside, he poured coffee for them both. Time to give her another little nudge and see what happened. "I thought I'd give Hakem a call."

Her cup rattled ominously in the saucer. "Why?"

Interesting. It would seem she didn't want him talking to his cousin. "To thank him, of course. What other reason could there be?"

Her eyes grew wary, the golds and greens muted into darkness. "Before you place that call, why don't you wait and make sure you have something to thank him for."

"You doubt your own suitability?"

"I think the next few days will answer that question. I recommend you wait until then." She pushed her cup aside and stood. "Ready to go?"

"You wish to leave?"

"I'm curious to see where you live."

"By all means." He gestured toward the door. "Let's satisfy your curiosity."

She'd only taken two short steps before she stopped and glanced at her feet, releasing a frustrated sigh. "Is it very far?"

"My car's parked in a garage beneath the building. But don't worry. You won't get your feet dirty."

He'd puzzled her with that one. "I won't?"

Before she realized what he intended, he swung her into his arms. Her breath escaped in a gasp of surprise that quickly turned to laughter. Something about the sound loosened the rigid control he'd maintained for more years than he could remember. As the future king of Rahman, duty, honor, and responsibility had been more important than any other qualities. After he'd left his homeland, that control had solidified, keeping him sane when fury and despair had threatened to engulf him.

But something about this woman—the vulnerability she couldn't quite conceal, the warmth and grace and sweetness that was such an innate part of her personality, the fullness of her passion—managed to slip beneath his guard. Right now he had her where he wanted her, safe and secure in his arms, her face tipped to his, full of light and laughter.

"If it means holding you like this, maybe I'll keep you barefoot forever," he warned roughly.

She didn't say anything in response. But her hands crept up his shoulders, linking around his neck, and she smiled before dropping her head to his shoulder. If he didn't know better, he'd swear she were shy. Cradling her close, he carried her from his office.

Home. It was time to bring his woman home.

*   *   *

Watching Zara invade his territory gave Malik an odd feeling. He'd have thought she'd look out of place in the strongly masculine setting. But instead it served to magnify her femininity. She was light surrounded by darkness, dainty elegance within stark simplicity. Taking her time, she explored room after room, a frown slowly forming between her brows.

"What's wrong?" he asked at length.

"This isn't at all what I expected."

"And that's not good, I assume."

Her frown deepened. "No, I don't think it is."

"It's getting late. Why don't I show you to your bedroom?" He opened a final door and gestured for her to enter. "At least...it's yours for the next day or two."

She didn't react to the suggestive comment. No blush. No start of surprise. No nervous retreat. He took up a stance in the middle of the doorway, trapping her in the room. "All right, Zara. I give up. Explain yourself." He folded his arms across his chest. "Why isn't my home what you expected?"

"I'm not sure...." She released her breath in a drawn-out sigh. "Oh, of course. Why didn't I see it before? There's nothing of Rahman here."

"No, there's not."

She turned to face him. "It's deliberate, isn't it?"

"Yes."

"But...why?"

"Because I don't want any reminders of all I gave up."

He despised the compassion that lit her eyes, despised even more that some small part of him might appreciate the comfort she instinctively offered. "I neither want nor need your pity," he bit out. "I made my peace with what happened in Rahman years ago."

"Have you?" she had the nerve to ask. "Or have you simply buried the pain? If you'd made your peace, wouldn't you take pleasure in a few prized mementos instead of wiping your home clean of your past?"

She'd touched on the untouchable and anger erupted, flaming hot and desperate. "You know nothing of the situation. Be smart, Zara. Let it go."

"I could prove it to you." Disregarding all sense of her own danger, she approached. "I could prove that Rahman still burns in your heart and soul, even after all these years."

He stopped her the only way he knew how. "You're here to share my bed, not my heart."

Even his harshness didn't faze her. She stepped closer, taking risks no woman had ever taken with him before. "I'm here to give you a gift."

"That gift is your body," he claimed, negating all his earlier reassurances. "Stick to that and we'll get along fine."

Still she didn't stop, brushing aside his comment with a graceful sweep of her hand. "Three days, Malik. Allow me three days to give you gifts of my choosing, gifts that will help heal the past."

"Is this how you follow Hakem's directions? As I recall you were to be polite, obedient and share my bed. So far you've failed on all counts."

She amazed him by shrugging off his fury. It didn't make a bit of sense. His passion frightened her, but his wrath didn't affect her in the least. This woman was a myriad of frustrating contradictions. "He also instructed me to give you a memorable birthday." A final step brought her within reach. She was either a very brave woman or a very foolish one. Considering how tenuous his control, he'd choose foolish. "Or are you afraid, Malik?"

"Watch yourself, woman." The very softness of his voice made the tone all the more lethal. It took every ounce of self-control to keep from snatching her into his arms and tossing her onto the bed. "You were sent for one purpose and one purpose alone. Push me and I'll see that you fulfill your duty."

A small tremor of awareness shivered through her. Or was it fear? Probably not, considering that she continued to confront him, refusing to use the least bit of common sense and back down. "If you truly have made peace with the past, why not let me help you celebrate your birthday my way?" she persisted. "Three short days. Is that so much to ask? You said you weren't looking for momentary pleasure. Prove it. Prove you're open to a more complete relationship."

"Fine. You have gifts you wish to give me?" He spread his arms wide. "Offer them now."

"I can't. They'll take time to prepare."

His arms dropped around her, caging her. She didn't resist his grasp, but continued to gaze up at him with a calm serenity he didn't have the heart to destroy. He didn't want her gifts, not if they involved Rahman. But he couldn't bring himself to refuse her. Not when she looked at him with such a devastating combination of trust and determination.

He'd intended to bring a fast end to the conversation. Instead he found himself inclining his head. "You need three days' worth of preparation time, I assume?"

"Yes."

"And after those days have passed?"

"I suspect we'll know each other rather well."

"Well enough to fulfill your obligations?" he demanded.

"If that's your wish." Her eyes glittered with hope. "Then you agree? You'll allow the gifts?"

"It would appear I don't have any other choice."

She shook her head, a tiny smile playing across her mouth. "None. Though, I have a final request."

Deciding caution would be a wise choice at this juncture, he gently propelled her out of reach and folded his arms across his chest once again. "You're pushing it, Zara."

"I know." She paced in front of him, threatening his hard-won sanity. Did she have any idea how her ivory skirt caressed her legs with each dancelike step she took? Or how the lamp behind her made the silk as transparent as her *abaaya*, allowing him to appreciate the shapely silhouette of her legs? "I need your secretary."

He deliberately returned his attention to her face. "You want to steal my secretary away from me?"

"Just borrow," she hastened to correct. "For a few hours, probably less."

"I know I'm going to regret asking… Why must you borrow her?"

"I'm new to this country and I'm not certain how to obtain everything I'll require. I thought she could advise me."

"I think that can be arranged." He lifted an eyebrow. "Anything else?"

She cleared her throat. "One other teeny, tiny detail."

"You don't know when to give up, do you?"

"No, but I gather it should be soon."

"Very soon." He fought for patience, an exercise in futility, he suspected. "What's the final detail?"

"Since King Haidar didn't authorize this—" she clasped her hands together, explaining delicately "—I don't have the means to arrange it."

"I'll tell Alice to authorize the expenditures. Will that do?"

"Yes, thank you."

"I trust you'll be reasonable in your purchases?"

"Absolutely."

"Are we through now? You've bargained all you intend to bargain?"

"Yes."

She wouldn't escape completely unscathed from their skirmish. He had some choice promises to extract, as well. "In that case, I want your word, Zara. Your word of honor. After the three days have passed, you'll put aside this foolishness and share my bed. That kiss we exchanged should be enough to convince you it won't be a hardship."

Her face paled. It would seem he'd struck the hardest bargain, after all. The knowledge surprised him. Why the virginal shock? Why the shy retreat? It didn't make any sense. "You...you have my word," she agreed after a momentary hesitation.

"Excellent. Your clothes will be brought up shortly. If there's anything else you need—"

"Save it until morning?" Zara suggested, recovering her poise.

A laugh broke from him. How had she managed that minor miracle? "It might be wise."

An answering smile quivered on berry-stained lips. "In that case, I'll see you in the morning," she assured solemnly. "You have my word on that, too."

"And are you always true to your word?"

He'd meant it as a joke. To his surprise, a shadow swept across her face and she winced. "No, I'm not." For the first time since she'd tumbled from the rug at his feet, her gaze evaded his. Taking a deep breath, she faced him once again, her expression resolute. "I didn't keep my word once just recently."

"Only once?" he asked gently.

"Yes, though I suspect I'll have to break my word one more time in the coming weeks. But I promise I'll always keep my promises to you. Will that be acceptable?"

Curiosity consumed him. He could see how much it disturbed her to have broken her word. So why had she done it when such an act clearly went against her ethical code? Whatever had prompted her decision, desperation must have played a vital role. He couldn't imagine any other reason she'd have made such a choice, though why he was so certain after such a short acquaintance, he couldn't say.

"Yes, Zara, it'll do," he soothed.

"I won't let you down."

"A wise decision." As a warning, it was relatively gentle. But he was satisfied to note that she took the admonition seriously. "Good night."

"Good night, Malik."

He stepped out of the room and closed the door, leaving Zara standing in the middle of the room. If she'd expressed the panic creeping into her expression with so much as a single word, he'd have swept her into his arms and carried her to bed, reassuring her in ways that would have put to rest her demand for a three-day grace period. And she would have been reassured, he'd have seen to that.

But she didn't say a word, didn't allow so much as a murmur to escape her lips. Regretfully he closed the door and stood in the hallway for a brief minute. So she'd decided to give him a gift. He shook his head. Didn't she realize that the only gift he wanted was her? What more could any man want?

Soon. Soon he'd explain that to her and she'd discover how foolish her fears had been. Soon he'd have her in his arms and in his bed. And it would be a long, long time before he let her go.

Zara had trouble unwinding, and she found herself pacing restlessly across the redwood floorboards. The clothes Malik had purchased for her were brought to the room by the housekeeper's teenage grandson, Benjamin, who'd smiled shyly before ducking from the room. The housekeeper, Mrs. Parker, was an older, no-nonsense woman who managed to thoroughly intimidate with a single look. But after a few minutes' conversation, she'd amazed Zara by thawing enough to offer an approving nod on her way out the door.

After sorting through the clothes, Zara put them away in the dresser drawers and in the closet. Next she showered and dressed in the simple sliplike nightgown. A half-moon shone in the window and she crossed the room to press her nose against the glass pane, staring out at San Francisco with a sense of acute wonder. She'd actually made it to the United States. She'd never expected to see her homeland. Not really. Her stepfather, Kadar, had been dead set against it, fearing she'd never return to Rahman once introduced to her native land.

His fears were justified. It wasn't that she'd wanted to leave Rahman, as much as she wanted to explore her roots. She'd also dreaded being forced into a loveless marriage. Although Kadar had promised that wouldn't happen, giving her to Hakem had proven too great a temptation, offering the opportunity to fulfill political aspirations that had festered for decades.

So now, instead of finding herself Hakem's wife, she would soon become Malik's mistress. She glanced over her shoulder at the bed and flinched. Soon. Soon she'd have no choice but to give him what he wanted. Just one short hour ago, she'd tried to ease her apprehension by considering the possibility of running away to escape her obligation. But now that she'd given her word, running was no longer an option.

Fear prompted her to race to the bed. She ripped off the comforter and flung it to the floor. Folding it in half lengthwise, she dumped pillows onto the makeshift mattress and last of all tugged free a blanket and sheet for a covering. She wasn't quite certain what she hoped to prove with her small act of defiance. But at least she wouldn't spend half the night obsessing over Malik and the eventuality of sharing her sleeping quarters with him.

Of course, within the hour she was proven wrong. The minute sleep claimed her, Malik stole into her dreams and into the privacy of her makeshift bed. Instead of his business suit, he wore a *thobe* and *gutra,* traditional robes and headdress. Pulling her into his arms, he covered her mouth with his, stealing her heart and soul with his kiss. And then he stripped away the silk slip covering her, baring her to his hungry gaze.

She'd expected to feel outraged, to fear his domination. Instead she wrapped her arms around his neck and willingly opened herself to his possession. His name was a plea on her lips, his touch as necessary to her as the air she breathed. And when he took her, the dream faded, leaving her aching for the completion she'd been denied.

In the wee hours of the morning, Zara crept into the bathroom and turned on the water in the shower stall full blast. She sat there, huddled beneath the hot, soothing spray until her last tear was spent.

"I'm telling you, she took that bed apart and slept on the floor. At least that's where she stayed when she wasn't in the bathroom. She must have showered for half the night."

Malik pushed aside coffee at that. "Half the night?"

His housekeeper nodded in confirmation. "I didn't think it was possible for a body to get so dirty. She didn't look all that bad when I delivered her clothes."

"No, she didn't."

"So explain why was she in the shower so long."

"I'll ask her when she comes down, Mrs. Parker."

"You mean, if she ever finishes showering, don't you?"

He sighed and pushed back from the table. "Why don't I go upstairs and find out what Zara's problem is."

"I'll tell you what her problem is." She slammed a silver coffeepot onto the table in front of him. "There's only one reason a woman stays in the shower that long."

"Please, Mrs. Parker. Enlighten me."

She folded her arms across her nonexistent chest. "It's a woman thing, Mr. Haidar."

Damn. "All the more reason you should explain it to me. I wasn't married long and the short year I was, my wife rarely took the time to educate me on these matters."

"Okay, fine. It's not something I like accusing a man of, but here it is…"

His brows drifted upward at that. "Accusing?"

"That's what I said. Accusing. Women sit in the shower like that when they're crying. There I said it." She shook her finger at him. "And shame on you for making that pretty little thing cry."

He didn't wait for her to say another word, but left the table. He took the stairs two at a time and strode down the hallway to Zara's bedroom. Lifting his fist, he hammered on the door.

CHAPTER FOUR

THE door opened almost immediately. Zara stood in front of him, her head tilted to one side in question. "Yes?"

To Malik's frustrated amusement, he found himself uncertain of what to say. He couldn't remember the last time that had happened with a woman. If she'd been crying in the shower all night, it wasn't apparent to him. Dressed in a pale green suit jacket and calf-length skirt, she looked cool and sophisticated and breathtakingly appealing. She'd pulled her magnificent hair into a loose knot at her nape and stared up at him with the clear, direct gaze that had haunted him through the endless night.

"Good morning," he said at last.

"I'm running late, aren't I?"

"Not too bad." He studied her cautiously. "Are you all right?"

"Fine, thanks. Why?"

"Mrs. Parker thought…" He shook his head. "Never mind. Are you ready for breakfast?"

"I still have one small problem." She glanced downward and wiggled her toes. "It's not that I mind going barefoot, you understand."

"But it might raise a few eyebrows if you left the house shoeless?"

She grinned. "Something like that. Or were you planning on taking care of it the same way you did yesterday?"

It was seven in the morning and the mere thought of carrying her in his arms as he had the night before was enough to have him urging her backward into the bedroom. "If I hadn't made a promise to you, we wouldn't be leaving this room anytime soon."

Her eyes widened slightly, glittering with the brilliance of liquid gold, enhanced by a green as pale and vibrant as her suit. A slight flush tracked across her cheekbones and he traced it with his fingertip. "But you did promise," she whispered.

"I know. But that doesn't mean I can't kiss you." He studied her face, determined to watch for the slightest change in expression, any nuance that might confirm his housekeeper's suspicions. "Or would you rather I didn't?"

Nervousness flickered across her features, along with a growing awareness. The nervousness he understood. They'd known each other less than a day and had been thrown into the most intimate of circumstances. The growing awareness pleased him since it precluded any hint of fear.

Her eyes darkened, the golds and greens taking on the shades of autumn, the color deeper and richer than any he'd seen before. The air shivered from her lungs in a silent sigh and her breasts rose and fell with each breath she drew. A longing eased into her expression and a softness touched her, a softness of face and form and intent. It was as though she cautiously unfurled beneath the heat of the sun, exposing her tender inner layers. In that instant he knew that she was taking a chance with him, risking the threat of a harsh scorching touch in the hopes of receiving a life-generating warmth.

He accepted the gift she offered. Filling his arms with

her he took her mouth with exquisite care. Her moan of pleasure rewarded him and her lips parted to allow him entry. He slipped inward, delighting in the taste and texture. Where had Hakem found someone so perfect? There was a sweetness to her rare in the women he'd known, a generosity of spirit he hadn't experienced for a long, long time.

He ran his hands the length of her back, the silk of her form-fitting suit jacket whispering a teasing plea. All he could think about was stripping away the garment and discovering what lay beneath. It wouldn't take much to send him over the edge. The woman in his arms had the uncanny ability to stir urges ungoverned by rational thought. He wanted her. He wanted her mind and her body, her laughter and her heart. He wanted to rip her hair free and feel it slide across his body as he possessed her.

But he wouldn't.

He'd promised to leave her untouched until three endless days had passed and he'd keep his word…even if it killed him.

She pressed her fingers to her mouth, taking a moment to recover. Of course, it took him every bit as long, he realized with a wry smile. "You stopped."

"Yes."

"I wasn't sure you would."

"I wasn't certain, either."

"But, you did."

"I promised," he explained simply. "I've been stripped of much, Zara. You know that. All I have left is my word. So I guard it well."

"Your word." For some reason, his comment disturbed her. A frown pulled her brows together and she grew still within his arms.

"Don't you believe me?"

"It's not that. You're...you're not the man I expected."

He understood then, and it explained so much. "You mean what you've seen of me doesn't match what you've heard. And what you've heard has frightened you."

"Yes."

"It would seem you have a problem." He refused to help resolve her dilemma, forcing her to reach her own conclusions. Deliberately he stepped away. "You're going to have to decide which is accurate... The stories you've heard or your own assessment of me."

"And if I'm a terrible judge of character?"

He leaned forward, interested to discover that she didn't pull back in alarm. Instead she swayed closer, as though waiting for a delicious secret to be whispered in her ear. "Then you're not just in trouble. You're in serious trouble."

Not waiting for her reaction, he turned and headed down the hallway. He hadn't taken more than two steps before she stopped him. "Malik, wait!"

He buried a smile and glanced over his shoulder. "What is it?"

"You've forgotten something."

"And what's that?"

She lifted her skirt an inch and stuck out her foot. A look of pure mischief lit her face. "No shoes."

He didn't say a word, but simply opened his arms. She flew into them and he scooped her high against his chest with a rough laugh. It felt good to laugh again. It had been a rare event before Zara's advent in his life.

But a single day with her and he found it all too easy.

As far as he was concerned, she'd given him his first gift.

"I realize I'll be invading your province, Mrs. Parker. That's why I wanted to check with you first." Zara tried to read the housekeeper's reaction, but the woman kept her thoughts as well hidden as Malik. "Would you mind sharing your kitchen?"

"Why?" the housekeeper asked suspiciously.

"It's a gift for Malik's birthday."

"His birthday's not until Friday. This is only Wednesday."

"I realize that. But I have a surprise for him each day leading up to his birthday. I need the kitchen for the first surprise."

Mrs. Parker shook her head. "I know you mean well, miss, but he's not going to like that. He hates celebrating his birthday."

"He hates his birthday?" How peculiar. "Why?"

"Can't say. He always has, at least for as long as I've been with him and that's going on nine years this September." She tasted the soup she was preparing and added a pinch of salt and a hearty helping of pepper. "We're not supposed to treat it as anything special. The only one who ever goes against Mr. Haidar's wishes is that cousin of his."

Oh, dear. That didn't sound good. "Well…" She offered the best excuse she had available. "Since I was sent by his cousin, I suppose I'm an exception, too."

"If you say so." Apparently Mrs. Parker didn't agree. "I can understand your wanting to celebrate on Friday. He'd probably put up with somebody forcing a special birthday dinner on him for a single day, especially a pretty thing like you. But for three days running?''

Zara grimaced. "Over the top?"

"I suspect we'll find out." The housekeeper transferred minced onions and garlic from her cutting board to a skillet. "Do these plans of yours mean you'll be messing around in my kitchen all those other days, too?''

"Not without your permission."

"I might consider allowing it." The woman turned her back on Zara to give the skillet a quick stir. "On one condition."

"What's the condition?"

"Explain why you were bawling your eyes out all last night."

Zara's breath caught. How in the world did Mrs. Parker know about that? She couldn't possibly have heard. "What makes you think I was crying?"

"You must have taken a half-dozen showers." The housekeeper spared a quick glance over her shoulder. "Can only mean one thing. Told Mr. Haidar so, too."

"You—" Zara closed her eyes, wincing. "You told Malik I was crying?"

"The minute I explained the facts to him, he hightailed it up the steps after you." She nodded in satisfaction. "It must have worked since he came down with you in his arms. Looked like a pair of newlyweds, if you want my opinion."

"I didn't have any shoes," Zara offered lamely. No wonder Malik had acted so strangely. "That's why he was carrying me."

"You think my floors aren't fit for your delicate feet? I'll have you know they're clean enough to—"

"Eat off of?"

The housekeeper's mouth twitched. "Heard that one before, have you?"

"Once or twice." Time for honesty. Zara sank into a seat at the sturdy kitchen table and traced her finger along a well-aged scar in the wood. "Would you care to hear the truth?"

"I wouldn't mind."

"I was crying because I was scared." Zara cupped her chin in her palm. "I've never been away from home before. And since I hadn't met Malik before coming here, I wasn't sure what to expect. He could have been a monster. And then where would I have been?"

"You didn't know Mr. Haidar before flying all this way?" Mrs. Parker asked in astonishment. "How's that?"

A bit of diplomatic evasion seemed wise. "I was sent by the King of Rahman—Malik's cousin—to give him his birthday present."

"So you said. And that's why you need my kitchen?"

"That's one of the reasons."

"I'm not sure I like the sound of this. A helpless, young woman handed over to an unmarried man by a king of some country I've never heard of. It's not respectable. What does your mother have to say about all this?"

She'd hit another sore spot. "My mother died a year ago."

"Now that's a shame. It surely is." Mrs. Parker's mouth pursed. "What do you suppose she'd say about this business if she were still alive? I find that's always a good way to judge what's right and what's not."

Zara lowered her gaze to the table again. "I suspect Mother would have a lot to say," she admitted.

The housekeeper nodded approvingly. "You've relieved my mind. At least you were brought up proper. Expect you'll make the smart choice once you've had time to give it a bit more thought."

Unfortunately she'd made a promise, which precluded that possibility. Zara pushed that particular worry from her mind in order to address her more immediate concern. "About using your kitchen..."

"It's yours if you want it."

Zara left the table to envelop the housekeeper in a hug. "Thank you, so much. I promise to leave it just as I found it."

"I would hope so." Mrs. Parker's tart tone belied the warmth with which she returned the hug. "I don't let just anyone rattle around in here, you know."

"I understand." Zara hesitated. "I do have one other small problem."

The housekeeper released an exaggerated sigh. "Spill it, girl. What now?"

"If I make up a list of ingredients and supplies, would you be able to tell me where to purchase everything?"

"The local grocer will have whatever you need."

"A grocer." Zara was intrigued. "I don't think I've ever been to one before."

"I wish I could say you were in for a treat."

"Oh! And Malik says my purchases must be 'reasonable.' Which reminds me... I'll need to mention that to Alice when I talk to her."

"Mr. Haidar's secretary?"

"Yes." Zara smiled in anticipation. "She's going to help me arrange for the birds, the goats—and cross your fingers—the camels."

* * *

"Zara?"

Malik closed the front door of his house and frowned at the absence of light and sound. If he didn't know any better he'd swear there was no one around. He'd half expected Zara to greet him at the door, barefoot and nimble, offering her first "gift."

He'd had his response already planned. If she still wore her hair up, he'd pull it loose, so it flowed down her back in a sheet of golden flame. Next, he'd take her in his arms and kiss her until he heard her tiny moan of pleasure, soft and urgent and totally unconscious. And then he'd carry her to his room and convince her that three days was an impossible length of time to wait, something neither of them truly wanted.

"Zara? Mrs. Parker?"

Pots and pans clattered in the distance and a steady stream of virulent Rahman drifted to him from the general direction of the kitchen. He grinned. For such an elegant thing, she had quite a colorful vocabulary. She appeared in the doorway between the dining room and the entranceway, covered in a voluminous apron, her fiery hair piled on top of her head. At some point it had begun to unravel and several long strands trailed down her back.

Seeing him, she glared. "You're early."

Her irritation amused him, though he did his best to hide that fact. Somehow he doubted she'd find anything humorous about her situation. Gazing at her, desire hit with unexpected force. Perhaps it was the generous dusting of flour on her nose or her disgruntled air. Or it could be her flushed cheeks and tear-bright eyes. Or maybe it was simply the way she danced in agitation. Something about her current appearance made him want to take her off to bed and soothe her ruffled nerves with a night of leisurely lovemaking.

His mouth twisted. Too bad she wouldn't feel the same way.

"To answer the questions you haven't asked, I'm three-quarters of an hour later than normal. A last-minute phone call kept me for which I apologize." He approached, taking his time. Tossing his suit jacket onto a dining-room chair, he loosened his tie. She bravely held her ground until he reached her side. Snagging her by the waist, he lifted her against him. "Hello, Zara. Did you miss me?" He leaned down to sample her mouth, giving free rein to his desire, if only for an instant.

He was pleased to see it took Zara a moment to recover her equilibrium. More telling than that, her agitation lessened within his arms, as though holding her eased her tension. The minute she recovered, though, she spun free.

"Where's Mrs. Parker?" he asked.

"Your housekeeper has the evening off." She shoved at her sagging topknot prompting several more long tendrils to tumble loose. "She and Benjamin are visiting relatives and won't be back until late."

"And what are you up to?"

A pungent aroma wafted from the direction of the kitchen, billowing in on a cloud of smoke. She fanned her hand through the air. "I'd think that would be self-evident. I'm burning dinner. Now, if you'll excuse me, I haven't finished charring it sufficiently."

Turning on her bare heel, she swept from the room. The door slammed behind her, then popped back open. "Please, have a seat. I'll be with you as soon as possible. And…'' Her chin shot up. ''And, yes, I missed you. Very much.''

He gave her two full minutes before walking into the kitchen and into sheer chaos. Pots bubbled over on the stove. Smoke roiled from a pan of some sort of unidentifiable meat. The sink was awash with dirty dishes. And the counters were generously dusted with flour and spices. Zara sat curled up in a chair at the table, her nose tucked into a cookbook.

''Problem?'' he asked dryly.

He'd startled her, and she snapped at him like a disgruntled terrier. ''I told you to wait.''

He shrugged off her protest. ''Since this is my home, I prefer making those decisions myself.'' He paused a beat before adding with gentle irony, ''I assume you don't object?''

Tossing the cookbook aside, she regarded him with open frustration. Then she buried her face in her hands, her shoulders trembling. He swore beneath his breath, furious with himself for reducing her to tears. ''Don't cry, Zara.'' Hastening to her side, he snatched her out of the chair and into his arms. ''Please, don't cry.''

She glanced up and he realized that she wasn't crying, but laughing. ''I'm sorry, Malik. I didn't mean to upset you. It's just…'' She gestured at the disaster area around her. ''Would you *look* at this place? Your housekeeper is going to kill me.''

His tension eased. ''Dinner not going as you planned?''

He'd actually managed to win a chuckle with that one. ''Does it smell like it's going well?''

''Not from my perspective. But since I don't know how to cook, I could be mistaken.'' Satisfied that he hadn't traumatized her, he released her and strolled toward the charred pan. "*Biryani,* perhaps?"

"What gave it away? The charred lamb or the burned rice?"

"And on the stove? Don't tell me that's *kibbe?*" A feeling of bittersweet longing seized hold, as intense as it was unexpected. "Where did you find the pine nuts?"

"At a local health food store. It was a fascinating place, though I hadn't realized we Americans were such a sickly lot. Mother never mentioned that."

So, she was American. That answered one of his questions about her. "I've found people here take their health quite seriously. Perhaps living in Rahman for so long, you avoided that particular predilection."

"I must have."

She didn't sound happy and he turned, offering her a sympathetic look. "Is there anything salvageable?"

"The salad. I made the *tabouli* nice and oily. Very traditional. The vegetables turned out all right. And believe it or not, the baklava didn't get ruined. So we can have dessert." She scowled. "It's just that darned stove. I couldn't get it to work right."

"Didn't you have one in Rahman?"

"We have one." A vivid blush bloomed across her checks. "I...I just didn't learn to cook on it."

Because they had servants? He suddenly realized how little he knew of Zara. He'd have to ask a few questions and hope she offered straight answers. "Where did you learn to cook?"

"Believe it or not, over an open fire." She grinned. "I could have made some very tasty dishes for you in your fireplace."

Malik could only stare, fascinated by her smile. What was it about her he found so appealing? Her hair drifted relentlessly southward and flour still powdered her nose, while Mrs. Parker's apron covered her more thoroughly than an *abaaya*. And yet, he found her every bit as enticing here and now as she'd been with a veil of thin black cotton covering her nudity.

He deliberately glanced away, before temptation got the best of him. "Perhaps we can salvage a bit of the lamb," he suggested. "Did you pick up any pita bread?"

She brightened. "Yes, I did. It doesn't taste quite the same as back home, but—"

"It'll do." He removed a sharp knife and fork from a drawer and crossed to the pan holding the lamb. "Let's see what I can rescue."

"While you take care of that, I'll put the rest of the dinner on the table."

"No, we'll eat in my study. It's less formal."

It didn't take long to move everything. He placed the various dishes on a low coffee table and tossed some throw pillows on the floor in place of chairs. Before he took his seat, he gathered Zara in his arms and kissed her again, more thoroughly this time.

"What was that for?" she asked when he released her.

"It's called a welcome home kiss. Consider it an American tradition." He picked up one of the linen napkins from the table and wiped the flour from her nose. "There's also a traditional after-dinner kiss, a before-bed kiss and a good-morning kiss."

She grinned. "That's a lot of tradition."

"Nowhere near enough, in my opinion." Reaching around her, he tugged at her apron strings. The covering sagged revealing the green suit she'd worn that morning, though she'd replaced the suit jacket with a long-sleeved silk shell in a wash of impressionistic pastels. He tossed the apron aside and removed the clip restraining her hair.

He found it interesting that she didn't object to his touch, but accepted it as his right. Would she have said something if she didn't like it, or would she simply have endured? His mouth tightened. He didn't want passive acceptance. He wanted her passion. Sensing his displeasure, she shot him a questioning look.

"Does my touch bother you?" he asked abruptly.

She couldn't fake such patent astonishment, nor the helpless desire that gleamed like gold in her eyes. "I don't mind."

"Would you tell me if you did?"

She gave it serious consideration. "Yes." She tilted her head to one side. "Would my objection change anything?"

"It would change everything," he replied simply. He gestured toward the cushions. "Come. Have a seat and tell me about your day."

Thrusting her hair away from her face, she pointed to their dinner. "You're looking at it."

"You worked on this the entire time?"

"I wanted you to have some typical dishes from home. What I hadn't counted on was that horrible stove."

She'd worked all day to bring him a taste of his homeland. He waited until he could be certain of his control before replying. "Thank you," he said formally. "It was a kind gesture."

"It was supposed to be more than a gesture. It was supposed to be eatable."

"Let's see if it isn't."

He reached for the first dish, but she stayed his hand

before he could remove the lid. "I fixed this as a gift for you. A poor one, true. Still... I'd like to serve you what there is."

"That's not necessary."

"Yes," she insisted gently. "It is."

She didn't give him the opportunity to argue. Kneeling, she removed the lid covering the vegetables and filled his plate with a generous portion. Giving in to the inevitable, he made himself comfortable and watched her.

Had someone taught her to be so graceful or had she been born with the ability? It seemed such an innate part of her personality, that he rather suspected her soul sang to some private, inner music. It was reflected in her every movement. From the way her hand seemed to flow from plate to bowl and back again, to the regal position of her head, to her smooth, dancelike stride, even to the stillness that occasionally came over her, it was as though she performed an unending ballet.

"Salad now or later?"

"Later. I'll have it with the cheese."

"How was your day?" She shook her head at her own question. "That sounds entirely too domesticated. How about this...? Tell me something about your day that no one else knows."

Interesting question. "That's a tough one. Alice is privy to all my business dealings, so there's not much she doesn't know."

"You must trust her."

"The business wouldn't be what it is without her."

"Ali and Jamil neglected to tell me about your work. Do you mind my asking?"

"Not at all." He scooped up a helping of lamb and

rice with the pita bread. "I'm a financier. I invest people's money."

"Is that what you were trained to do?"

"I was trained to rule a country." At her stricken look, he relented. "But the economics of running an entire country can be applied to my current career. It's not quite as complicated, but it's an interesting enough challenge."

She recovered swiftly. "You still haven't told me something about your day that no one else knows."

"I could say I thought about you."

"Is it the truth?"

"You were never far from my thoughts."

He hadn't pleased her. Her expression cooled and she assumed an even more regal posture. "You don't have to seduce me, Malik. That part is a given, remember? I don't require mindless flattery or false declarations."

"Then I won't offer them."

He selected a morsel of lamb that had escaped the worst of the heat. He offered her the tidbit, curious to see whether she'd accept or scorn his gift. To his secret pleasure, she took it without a qualm, even daring to lick the juice from his fingertips.

"Thank you," she said, the prim tone ruined by the huskiness of her voice.

"I thought about Rahman," he surprised himself by admitting. "And I wondered what you planned to do to prove that my homeland still has any meaning to me."

He'd shocked her. "Do you really think it doesn't?"

"I don't think. I know." He gestured toward the dishes spread before them. "You were kind to fix this, Zara, but it won't change my mind. I lost the part of myself that was Rahman ten years ago. There's no going back."

"I'm not suggesting you go back. I'm trying to show you that it still has a place in your heart."

"It's a cold place."

"But it doesn't need to be."

"Let it go." His warning cut sharper than he'd intended and he deliberately wiped all emotion from his voice before continuing. "What does it matter, Zara? You're here for a short time. Let's enjoy the moments we have together."

"Keep it light and meaningless? Is that how you prefer your women?"

"Somehow I suspect you couldn't do 'meaningless' if your life depended on it." He deliberately edged the conversation in a new direction. "You must have had an unusual upbringing."

She answered his probing with a shrug. "With the exception of my mother, I was the only girl in a household of men."

"The youngest?"

"Yes."

"The adored sister and daughter?"

She smiled. "To a certain extent. I had a lot of trouble learning appropriate behavior. I was always a bit too exuberant."

He eyed her keenly. "I trust they responded with indulgent exasperation?"

"Is that your way of asking if I was mistreated?"

"I suppose it is."

"I wasn't mistreated."

"But they wouldn't approve of you being here, would they?"

She hesitated for a long moment before reluctantly shaking her head. "No, they wouldn't."

"Then why are you?"

"Because I want to be." Her hand fluttered through the air. "Because it offered opportunities unlike anything back home. And because it gave me the chance to see where I was born."

"Should I be worried that an army of outraged brothers will show up on my doorstep out for my blood?" It was a throwaway question, and yet it impacted like a blow. She jumped to her feet and began collecting dirty dishes. Most telling of all, she avoided his gaze. "Zara?" His voice hardened. "Should I be worried?"

"Trust me, if my brothers showed up on your doorstep, I'd be more shocked than you."

With that, she swept from the room, leaving him staring after her with narrowed eyes. He'd ignored that feeling of "wrongness" ever since she'd arrived. But it was beating at his consciousness now, breaking through the barriers of desire and personal preference to shout a loud warning. Something about this situation didn't ring true and he'd better find out what…and why.

The time had come to call Hakem.

CHAPTER FIVE

MALIK waited until Zara had left the room to prepare coffee and dessert before placing the call. To his surprise, his request to speak to his cousin was instantly granted.

"Do you have any idea what time it is?" Hakem growled into the receiver.

"I gather you were already up or they wouldn't have put through the call."

"I wouldn't be, except we have a bit of a situation here."

Malik straightened. "What is it?"

"Kadar. Who else?"

"What's he done this time?"

"You're not going to like this." Hakem released his breath in a long sigh. "He gave me his daughter as my future bride."

It took a moment to digest that. So far, Hakem's union with Rasha had only been blessed with daughters. If Hakem married Kadar's daughter, and she produced a son, the boy would most likely become the heir apparent. It would put Kadar in a dangerous position of power. "Very clever. I see the bastard hasn't lost his touch."

"He's as shrewd as ever. He presented me with her in a way that made refusing impossible without giving insult."

"How's Rasha taking it?"

"As well as can be expected. It doesn't help that this has happened so near the end of her pregnancy."

"I imagine not. Any chance she can give you a son before you're forced to marry this girl? When's the wedding scheduled to take place?"

"That's a little difficult to say. My precious bride-to-be has disappeared. That's the crisis."

Malik released an incredulous laugh. "You're kidding."

"I wish I was. I have every one of Kadar's relatives camped around the palace making threats of death and destruction. They think I've done something to her in order to avoid the marriage."

It sounded like an explosive situation, possibly as explosive as the one he'd found himself in ten years earlier. "So what really happened to her?"

"I don't think she wanted the marriage and took off at the first opportunity."

"She had the nerve to defy Kadar?"

"You'd have to meet her to understand. She's... unusual."

Which reminded him. "So is the woman you sent. My thanks, by the way."

"Believe it or not, my bride-to-be selected her."

"You allowed—"

"Kadar's daughter to choose. Amusing, yes?"

Malik's breath escaped in a disbelieving laugh. "No wonder the girl ran off. You probably offended her."

"Not this one. She's not from—" Irate voices sounded in the background. "Listen... I have to go. Kadar's arrived."

"Don't agree to anything until you find the girl," Malik advised. "You might be able to turn this to your advantage, yet. Perhaps she ran off with a lover. That would take care of Kadar's plans once and for all."

"We couldn't be so lucky." Hakem hesitated. "I wish we had more time to talk. Happy birthday, cousin. Enjoy my gift."

"I intend to. You don't have any objection to my keeping her for a while, do you?"

"She pleases you that much?"

"More."

"Then, she's yours as long as you want her."

"I was hoping you'd say that."

"I'm delighted I could find something to your liking. It's been ages since I've heard you sound so contented."

"I am." And it was true, Malik realized in surprise. In the short time Zara had been with him, she'd given him that much. Amazing.

"Listen," Hakem interrupted. "We'll talk again as soon as I've settled this matter."

"I'll be interested to hear what happens."

With a final farewell, Malik disconnected the call and tossed the phone aside, analyzing all the possible consequences of Hakem's situation. Deliberately he set aside his concerns. Rahman's problems were no longer his. Kadar had put an end to that when he'd won their long-ago battle. Malik could only hope his cousin was smarter at avoiding the traps their nemesis had prepared than he had been.

The door opened and Zara entered carrying a tray of coffee and baklava. Malik crossed the room and took it from her, realizing that he'd neglected to ask Hakem more questions about her. Unfortunately it would have to wait until this latest crisis had ended. Though now that he thought about it, his questions may have already been answered. If Kadar's daughter had selected Zara, that might explain a lot. Instead of choosing a more experienced companion, she'd selected someone far different from the norm. Hakem had said his bride-to-be was unusual. Perhaps she'd chosen someone like herself, if such a thing were possible.

He grinned. Who'd have imagined? He might have something to thank Kadar for, after all.

"I see him! He's just pulled in." Zara clapped her hands. "Places everyone."

"Zara? There's a problem," Benjamin began.

"Is it something Mrs. Parker can deal with?"

"My grandmother said you have to handle it."

Zara peered through one of the stained-glass windows flanking the front door. The beveled glass split the image, distorting her view. Through the soft rose glow of one of the panels, she could make out Malik climbing from his Jag and pulling a briefcase from the back seat. He stood and looked at it for a minute before tossing it back into the car and slamming the door closed. She grinned. It would appear she'd made an impact, if only a small one. Work would stay at the office.

"Miss Zara?" Benjamin prompted. "The problem?"

She waved him off. "Malik's coming up the walk. I'll deal with whatever it is later."

"But—"

The door handle rattled and muttering beneath his breath, Benjamin hastened from view. An instant later Malik stepped across the threshold and stopped dead. "What the—"

Zara stared at him anxiously. "Do you like it? I spent all day getting it just right. And see? I'm here to greet you at the door for your traditional welcome-home kiss.''

He made no move to claim his kiss. Closing the door with deliberate care, he examined her latest ''gift,'' a muscle leaping in his jaw. ''What have you done to my home?'' he asked with a softness that impacted like a rifle shot.

''It's all rented. But only for the day.'' She clasped her hands together. Did he love it? Hate it? After his first stunned look, his expression had closed over, making it impossible to read. ''Tomorrow it'll be gone again. But it's all ours for tonight.''

''What have you *done?*''

Oh, no. He hated it. ''I...I tried to duplicate your palace in Rahman,'' she whispered. ''What I could remember of it, that is.''

No doubt she'd forgotten some details, but she'd done her best. The entranceway was overflowing with plants of all descriptions, just like the palace. And just like the palace, two huge golden leopards with emerald eyes and onyx spots guarded the door. Of course, the Rahman leopards were decorated with real gem stones, instead of glass imitations. Unfortunately, attempting to rent something that valuable for a day would have fallen far from the realm of what Malik deemed ''reasonable.''

Other items she'd used, particularly the ferns, weren't native to Rahman. But the greenhouses and florists she'd contacted couldn't manufacture what they didn't have, particularly on such short notice. So she'd duplicated the general appearance as closely as possible.

To her delight, the antique stores had been better stocked. Huge brass urns, delicate figurines, teak tables and richly colored handwoven rugs overran the foyer.

And she'd prepared one further surprise. Rasha had told her that Malik's mother had been an avid birder, who'd kept an extensive aviary. Maybe the ones supplied by the pet shop would bring back special memories—memories he'd done his best to suppress. Of all her finds, she was proudest of the huge green-and-blue parrot that sat on an open perch by the door to the study, watching them with a bright, curious gaze. He was identical in every way to Cash-Cash, the parrot that greeted guests arriving at the palace.

Continuing to examine the entranceway, Malik thrust a hand through his hair, his expression settling into grim lines. "This looks like the palace."

"That's what I just said. I did my best to copy it." She studied him uneasily. "I thought—"

"No, Zara. You didn't think," he interrupted harshly. "If you had you'd never have—"

A loud, inhuman shriek resounded from the depths of the house, interrupting him, followed by an infuriated shout that could only have come from Benjamin. Sure enough he appeared at the end of the hallway, searching frantically among the various plants and potted trees.

Zara took a step toward him. "Benjamin? What in the world?"

With another shriek, a peacock exploded from a clump of ferns, trailed by a harem of squawking peahens. They raced in frantic circles, successfully evading Benjamin's efforts to contain them, before disappearing in the direction of the kitchen.

"You brought peacocks into my house?"

Oh, dear. Malik didn't sound the least pleased. She hurried to explain. "They're supposed to be in the courtyard. I guess this is the little problem Benjamin tried to tell me about."

"A neighboring cat came to investigate," the teenager interrupted. "I thought they'd be safer inside. I had them in the laundry room, but my grandmother opened the door and—" He shrugged, mischievous laughter vying with chagrin. "They knocked her clean off her feet. She was *not* happy."

Malik's dark eyes glittered with barely suppressed fury. "That makes two of us. Get the birds back into the laundry room. And then call the person responsible for their care and arrange for their immediate return. Do I make myself clear?"

"Yes, sir," Benjamin murmured, before hastening after the fleeing peacocks.

Zara's enthusiasm ebbed. It was clear she'd made a mistake trying to duplicate Malik's palace, even though she'd meant well. She gestured halfheartedly toward the study. "Why don't we go in there until dinner is ready."

"Should I expect more surprises?"

"One or two," she murmured. Or maybe, six or seven.

"Am I going to like them any better than the ones I've seen so far?"

"I doubt it."

He gave a stoic nod. "Then I'll be prepared." He faced the study, as though it were his execution. "Lead the way."

The parrot squawked as they approached. *"There was a young lady from Venus,"* he shrieked at the top of his lungs. *"Whose nose was shaped like a—"*

To Zara's surprise, Malik grabbed her arm and thrust her into the room, slamming the door closed on the final word. "He talks," she informed Malik, hoping he'd be impressed. "Isn't that nice?"

"Just great." He cocked his head to one side and listened. "He also swears like a sailor."

"Oh." She shot him a look every bit as mischievous as Benjamin's. "I wouldn't have noticed. The only bad words I know are in Rahman."

"Trust me. His vocabulary is even more extensive than yours in that department."

Zara stepped out of his way and allowed him to examine the study. She'd done a little transforming in this room, as well. Delicate wrought-iron cages filled with birds hung from stands around the room. Finches trilled, lovebirds cooed, cockatiels whistled and conures chattered. As background noise, Zara found it a bit overwhelming. But she had to admit, the birds were delightful to watch and occasionally hold.

As for the rest of the room, she'd done her best to keep everything light and airy, and overflowing with color. From the bolts of jewel-bright silk covering the furniture, to the contrasting pillows topping the silk throws, to the delicate curtains covering the windows, Zara had attempted to copy the room she'd stayed in during her brief stint at the palace.

"I know this place," he murmured. He crossed to a small end table that held a music box. Opening it, strains of Schumann's *Träumerei* filled the air. "And I remember this. It was years ago. When I was a little boy."

"Do you remember who it belonged to?" she asked gently.

"My mother—" He broke off, his mouth compressing. When he spoke again, his voice rasped, harsh with emotion. "It belonged to my mother."

"I spent the night in her room. Rasha told me they've kept it the same as when your mother was alive. They use it for guests now, guests who can get to know her through the personality of her room.''

It took him a long moment before he'd gathered himself enough to speak. ''You met Rasha?''

''Yes. She's a lovely woman.''

''She would have been offered to me as my second wife, if circumstances had been different.''

''So I was told.'' But when Rasha had said it, Zara had felt nothing but distaste. Since meeting Malik, a different feeling possessed her. One she had no business experiencing. ''Would you have liked being married to her?''

''She's Hakem's wife. What I would like has no bearing on the situation.''

Zara couldn't help pushing. ''Is she one more regret, Malik?''

He closed the music box with a gentle hand and fixed his dark gaze on her. ''She is not.''

''That's good.'' Zara managed a smile. ''I'd have had the most awful time trying to duplicate her.''

A low, husky laugh escaped him. ''It might have been amusing to see you try.''

She'd wanted so much to please him and she'd failed utterly. ''I'm sorry if I've upset you. It wasn't my intention.''

''I know.'' He crossed to another table overrun with a collection of bells. He picked them up one by one, ringing each in turn. ''She loved bells,'' he murmured. ''Bells and running water. I'd almost forgotten. She said they made happy sounds. Mother was always looking for happy sounds. Maybe it was because she was sick for so long.''

''How old were you when she died?''

''Five.''

"I was four when I lost my father."

A moment of perfect understanding passed between them, a connection forged through sorrow and bittersweet memories. "It's not pleasant to lose a parent, is it?"

She shook her head. "No, it's not."

Malik turned his attention to the table again. An ornate glass perfume bottle rested in the middle of the bells and he picked it up, removing the stopper. A heady mixture of sandalwood, citrus and honeysuckle filled the air and he closed his eyes with a low groan.

"Was it hers?" Zara asked.

"Yes. She always smelled of perfume. It was one of her defining qualities." The words were dragged from him, acute sorrow mingling with a fierce love. "Hugging her was like embracing a flower garden. We grieved so when she died."

"That's when you learned to close yourself off from bad memories, wasn't it? To wipe them from your mind as though they never existed. To lose the good with the bad."

He didn't deny it. "It seemed easier that way."

"Easier to lose your mother completely? Is that what you still think?" She allowed the idea to settle in his mind before continuing. "I wish I'd met her. Anyone who inspired such love must have been a special woman."

"She'd have liked you."

"Really?" The suggestion pleased her. "Why do you think that?"

"She liked color, whether it was in her decorations or her clothing or the people she met." He faced her. "And your personality is filled with color."

For some reason his comment brought tears to her

eyes. "Thank you," she whispered. "That's the nicest thing you've ever said to me."

"No, Zara. Thank you." He replaced the perfume bottle and approached. His hands settled on her shoulders and he drew her close, dropping a tender kiss on her forehead. "I was wrong and you were right."

"About what?"

"About remembering my past. I allowed the bad memories to steal away the good."

Two days worth of tension drained from her. Perhaps her gifts had done their job, after all. "You left good memories behind in Rahman, didn't you?" she prompted.

"Many good memories." He glanced around the room. "This was one of my favorites."

"Then I'm glad it's the one I chose."

He urged her closer, smiling in amused exasperation. "What am I going to do about you?"

"You're going to enjoy the gifts I give you. You're going to enjoy the time we have together." She forced herself to finish, to say the words that hurt more than she'd have thought possible. "And after we part, you'll hold those memories close, instead of locking them away."

His amusement faded. "What if I don't want us to go our separate ways?"

"Do you expect me to stay as your mistress, Malik?"

"Isn't that why you're here?"

She yanked free of his grasp, turning sharply away. To hear it stated so bluntly sounded obscene in the beauty of the room she'd created. It was an offense to his mother, as well as to herself. It also shredded the last of her romantic illusions. He was right. She hadn't come to gift him with pleasant memories of Rahman, but to gift him with her body. This wasn't a courtship, but a seduction. There wouldn't be anything honorable about the night she went into his arms. Her motives might justify her actions, but the path she'd chosen wasn't one she'd remember with pride. His reminder had brought that home, as had his assumptions that she'd willingly remain as his mistress.

"Zara? Zara, look at me."

She bowed her head, a swath of hair tumbling forward to conceal her discomfort from his keen gaze. "I can't."

"Why?" She felt his touch again, the warmth and strength and power that were such a natural part of him. "Why can't you look at me?"

Shame filled her. "I'm not the sort of woman who would make a good mistress."

"I don't understand. Zara, turn around and tell me what's going on."

She did as he asked, helpless to resist his entreaty. Perhaps if he'd been harder, rougher, she could have refused. But not when such warmth edged his voice. "I'm your birthday gift, Malik. That's all. Don't ask me to be more than that."

"Do you have other commitments? Is there someone else?"

He'd phrased it so carefully, and yet it might as well have been a slap. What he meant was...did she have another man waiting for her services? "No. There's no one else." Nor would there ever be. Not after Malik.

"Then what?"

How could she explain that while she'd revel in his possession, that some core part of her would die a painful death at the manner in which she'd given herself to him? To do so would ruin everything she was trying to accomplish by coming here. He was waiting for an answer and she scrambled for a believable explanation. Perhaps she could offer a different truth, one that wouldn't require such a painful confession. One that wouldn't involve her admitting how ashamed she'd be to live her life as a man's plaything.

"I can't stay because after I'm through here, I plan to find my family."

She surprised him with that one. "Your family?"

"My parents were Americans, Malik. Although I was raised in Rahman, I was born in this country and I have a grandmother and aunts and uncles and cousins who live here. I'm hoping to find them."

Comprehension dawned. "That's why you agreed to this, isn't it?"

"That was part of the reason. But only part," she hastened to add.

"What was your other reason?" Anger sparked in his eyes. "Explain why you're willing to give yourself to me once, but not stay and enjoy what we have together."

"I can't explain, other than to say that it's for a good reason."

He glared in frustration. "Does Hakem know this reason?"

Mutely she shook her head, struggling to hide the nervous dread his question provoked.

"Would he approve?"

Finally. A question she could answer. "He would approve of the results. And he would understand my reasons."

"Fair warning. I expect truth between us, not word puzzles. I don't like this game you play."

"And I don't like playing games. I'm not good at them."

"No, you're not. You don't have the panache to pull off a good lie."

She inclined her head in agreement. "Which is why I find honesty the better option. Unfortunately this is one situation where I can't give you the unconditional truth. It isn't my place." Hoping to offer some small gesture of comfort for her obstinence, she touched his arm. "Malik, please. Can't we simply continue as intended? Tomorrow's your birthday. I have one final surprise for you."

"Will you stay longer than tomorrow?"

She softened. "If that's your wish. I can stay a little longer. But then I'll want to look for my relatives."

He didn't argue further. "Why don't I have Alice help? You can give her whatever information you have about your family. As soon as she's located them, I'll take you for a visit."

"That's not necessary."

"Yes, it is." His tone was adamant. "I'm not comfortable with the idea of your wandering around the countryside searching for long-lost relatives. Once they've proven to my satisfaction that they really are your family and that they'll welcome and care for you, I'll let you go."

She didn't bother arguing. In the few days she'd known him, she'd learned to respect that steely undertone. "And in the meantime?"

"In the meantime, we'll enjoy what we have together."

At least he hadn't threatened to call Hakem. Nor had he threatened to return her to Rahman. Instead he'd offered his assistance in finding her family. How different

Malik had proven to be than the man she'd expected. Direct, honorable, honest. This wasn't a murderer, regardless of what Kadar and her stepbrother Paz had claimed. She struggled to reconcile the two images in her mind, before giving it up. Something had happened ten years ago. Something terrible. Whatever it was, she didn't have a hope of figuring it out. Not in the short time she had remaining.

As for tomorrow...

She set her chin. Her plans had been made, her final gift already in the works. Tomorrow would also put an end to her stepfather's scheme. When the moment came to give herself to Malik, she'd do it without hesitation. Knowing him, it would prove to be an unforgettable evening, one that would live long in her memory and in her heart. Anticipation shivered through her, catching her by surprise. Surely she couldn't have come to care for Malik to the point of romanticizing their coming encounter? But no matter how hard she tried, she couldn't escape the truth. Somehow that was precisely what she'd done.

In two short days, Malik had become her universe.

"What is it, Zara?" He cupped her chin and lifted her face to his. "What are you thinking about?"

"Tomorrow night," she answered candidly.

"They looked like pleasant thoughts."

"They were."

She expected to see masculine satisfaction appear on his face. Instead, tenderness burned in his eyes, along with an unmistakable passionate warmth. "You know I'll do whatever it takes to make sure the reality matches your anticipation."

"I don't expect you to match it."

He lifted an eyebrow. "You don't?"

"Oh, no," she teased. "I expect you to exceed it."

"What do you mean she's not here?" Malik demanded.

"I'm sorry, Mr. Haidar," Mrs. Parker retorted. "Saying it twice isn't going to change the facts. Zara's gone off, but she left you this note."

Dread burrowed deep into his gut. She'd run. He'd known she was nervous, that being given to a man as though she were some sort of love slave went against her nature. But he'd thought they'd gotten past that. He'd been careful not to make demands, to allow her to decide whether to stay or return to Rahman. After their conversation yesterday, he'd assumed she wasn't just willing, but anticipating tonight. Apparently fear had won out over trust.

He took the note without a word and walked to his study. Closing the door behind him, his gaze moved slowly over the room. The decorations from the previous day had been stripped away, as Zara had promised. All except a single brass bell, the music box identical to his mother's and the faintest trace of sandalwood and honeysuckle that lingered in the air.

Glancing at the note, he realized he'd crushed it in his fist. One by one, he unclenched his fingers. How had she managed to slip beneath his guard? He'd worked hard to protect himself from his past. From memories of Rahman. From women in general. But somehow, in three short days, she'd whirled into his life and worked a potent magic. She'd haunted his days with her thoughtful "gifts" and haunted his nights with images of serene hazel eyes that saw far too much of what he preferred to keep hidden. With her graceful dancer's body, pale silken skin and eager kisses, she'd offered a fantasy he'd found irresistible.

A fantasy that wasn't to be his.

He inhaled sharply. Enough. If she'd left, so be it. He'd told her countless times before that he didn't take unwilling women. And even though he wanted this one more than any who'd come before, he wouldn't force her into his bed.

Ripping apart the envelope, he removed the single sheet of paper and braced himself to read her words of farewell. Instead of a letter full of apologies and remorse, there were three short lines. They were directions, as clear and straightforward as the woman who'd written them. A rumble of laughter drifted up from deep within his chest, the sound less rusty than usual.

He stopped by the kitchen to inform Mrs. Parker of his plans. "I don't know when we'll be back."

"Not until late tomorrow, according to Miss Zara. I believe she arranged with your secretary to free up your schedule."

"Has she now."

"Your guest is quite an industrious young lady." His housekeeper flashed Malik a quick smile. "And kind-hearted. She's worked hard on these gifts of hers, trying to find bits and pieces that would please you. With the exception of that disgraceful parrot, I'd say she's succeeded."

"Yes, she has." Even the "disgraceful" parrot had given him a chuckle. "She's...a surprise."

"A welcome surprise, I hope?"

"Very welcome," he confirmed softly. "If you'll excuse me. I have an appointment to keep."

"Have a happy birthday, Mr. Haidar," she dared to say.

"I intend to." For the first time in a very long time, he'd find his birthday an occasion to celebrate, rather than a day spent reliving one of the darkest moments in his life.

"Oh, I forgot to tell you," she called after him. "That cousin of yours telephoned. He said—"

Malik nodded impatiently and kept going. "I'll call him back tomorrow."

"But he said it was urgent," she finished. Realizing her employer had left without hearing the end of the message, she shook her head in exasperation. "I assume urgent can wait until tomorrow, too. I declare, that girl has you wound up like a toy soldier and marching to her personal drumbeat. Bet my last bit of soup stock I'll be calling her Mrs. Haidar before the month's out. I'm gonna win that bet, too. Sure as I'm standing here talking to myself."

CHAPTER SIX

THE drive to Zara's "gift" took Malik a full hour and a half and he fought to keep from taking his impatience out on the gas pedal. Picking up a speeding ticket wouldn't get him to his destination any faster. Checking the directions he'd been given, he turned off the freeway and followed a back road into the mountains. The last part of the trip took him into a wide valley where mountain runoff had been dammed to form a small lake. Some industrious soul had spread white sand beside the lake for a beach and a huge Bedouin-style tent had been set up in the sand, along the shoreline.

Parking the car a short distance away, he walked to the campsite. A large fire crackled cheerfully in front of the tent, a chicken browning on a spit over the flames. It smelled delicious, but he was more interested in finding Zara. Pulling aside the flap to the tent, he was surprised to discover it empty.

Still, he could see Zara's unique handiwork on the decorations. Some of the plants she'd used to transform his hallway the day before had been placed in the corners of the tent. Rugs covered the sand and silk pillows formed couches. Color abounded. Neatly displayed in the middle of the tent was a *thobe* and *gutra*, Rahman dress he hadn't worn in ten long years. Where had she found the clothing?

He approached, examining the robe more closely. The collar of the *thobe* was identical to the ones he'd worn at the palace, while the embroidery along the edges of the *gutra* indicated the owner of the head scarf was a member of the ruling family. Most telling of all, the *agal,* the gold head ropes used to secure the *gutra* in place marked him as a prince.

Did she expect him to change into this? Didn't she realize how painful that would be? He stood, debating for a full five minutes. Just as he was about to leave the tent and confront her over the issue, he caught the unmistakable blend of honeysuckle, citrus and sandalwood. It was as though his mother's essence had come to him on a desert breeze from ages long past.

He closed his eyes, accepting a truth he'd spent a full decade denying. Regardless of all that had transpired, these garments symbolized his heritage. He'd been born and raised in the palace of Rahman. He'd descended from kings. His blood was Rahman. His heart beat in time with the pulse of his country. And his soul had been forged in the heat of the desert, beneath a burning sun. He could no more remove that part of himself than Zara could deny her American heritage. How had one so young become so wise? She'd known instantly what it had taken him years to understand.

He couldn't move forward until he'd accepted his past.

Taking a deep breath, he dressed in the garments she'd provided, amazed that in such a short time she'd turned his world upside down. If someone had told him he'd enjoy a Rahman meal, actually appreciate having his home transformed into a duplicate of the palace he'd been forced to leave and don garments he was no longer entitled to wear, he'd have ripped them apart. Yet with a sunny smile spread across her delectable mouth and a vulnerable innocence glistening in her hazel eyes, she'd convinced him to grant her every whim—no matter how much he'd have preferred to refuse.

The delicate chiming of bells and distant chatter of voices drew his attention to the campfire outside. Leaving the tent, he found Zara waiting for him. But it was a Zara unlike any he'd seen before. This woman was exotic and sensual. Instead of diaphanous black, she wore sheer emerald green. Her veil did little to conceal her hair and face, merely softened them with a nearly transparent wisp of green that was held in place by a silver *ilagah*. The braided chains circled her forehead and tumbled down her back and were covered in silver bells that sang out with her slightest movement.

Her caftan was almost as sheer as her veil. If it weren't for the colorful embroidery—a peacock, he realized in amusement—she'd have been bared to his gaze. Only the bird's plumage preserved her modesty. The peacock's head skimmed low over her breasts, while the colorful feathers curved across her belly to flare dramatically at her hips and upper thighs.

She became a concert of silvery sound and seductive movement, drawing his eye with each twist of her body. The peacock appeared to flutter in response, allowing tantalizing glimpses of soft, creamy skin—the generous curve of her breast, the narrow indent of her waist, the womanly flare of her hips, and the shadowy triangle at the apex of her thighs.

Desire hit hard, raging with primitive need. It took every ounce of willpower to control the masculine instinct to take and possess, to suppress the urge to mate. He forced his gaze away from her. Soon. Soon he'd stake a claim no one would dare violate.

Tonight, nothing would prevent him from making her his.

He looked around, surprised to discover that in the short time it had taken him to change, other tents and campfires had sprung up, though they occupied spaces at a discreet distance from the one he shared with Zara. The camp was decidedly Bedouin in appearance. His wasn't the only *thobe*, though he could spot every design from Saudi to Bahrain to several light blue *dishdasha* from Oman. Children raced from one site to the next, laughing and playing. Goats rambled around the outskirts of the area while chickens scratched in the dirt.

"All that's missing are the camels," he eventually commented.

"I tried to get them, as well." Her mouth turned down. "But Alice said the price was unreasonable."

"Remind me to give her a bonus when I return to work."

Even across the span of the fire, he could see the laughter gleam in her bewitching eyes, the dramatic sweep of kohl lining her lids emphasizing the unusual color. "I believe she's taken care of that, too."

He drew in a deep breath, aware of an underlying contentment. "Do you know how many years it's been since I was last in the desert?"

"Ten?"

Her gentle compassion was a balm to his pain. "Ten and a half," he replied. Had it really been that long? Some days it felt like he'd just left Rahman. On others it felt as if he'd been gone an eternity. "Most people I knew usually went 'wadi bashing' in a Jeep. But when it came to exploring the desert, Father preferred following the old ways."

"If I'd made you take a camel, you wouldn't have gotten here for ages," Zara pointed out with indisputable logic. "Besides, this isn't the desert, no matter how hard I tried to make it one."

No, it wasn't. "It's rocky enough. But too many trees."

"It's not hot or dry enough, either," she added.

"And the sounds and odors are all wrong."

Bells stirred to vibrant life as she circled the fire toward him. "But we can pretend, can't we?"

"Yes. We can pretend." She was as beautiful as she was generous. Once he made her his, how would he ever let her go? "You've gone to a lot of trouble. Thank you."

"It's my pleasure."

In a purely possessive gesture, he tugged the lower half of her veil so it sagged beneath her chin. "I don't even want that much concealing you from me," he informed her roughly.

"Then it won't."

"Don't make me wait, Zara. Kiss me. Kiss me like you mean it."

She shook her head, a smile playing at the corners of her mouth. "Don't you know? Haven't you figured it out?"

He released his breath in a gruff sigh. "Apparently not."

"I've always meant it." She reached up and wrapped her arms around his neck. "Every kiss was an honest expression of how I felt. I haven't lied to you, Malik. And I never will."

She sealed her vow by joining her mouth with his. He could feel the eagerness in her, taste the intimate surrender of her passion. She invaded his mouth, all moist heat and burning sweetness. No, she hadn't lied. She wanted him. There was too much of herself in her kisses for him to doubt the truth. She gave him everything, holding nothing back. He cupped her face, caressing her jawline with his thumbs. A moan rippled through her and he inhaled it, took it deep into his lungs so it would be part of him.

It was like having her inside him.

Gently he set her from him. "No more. Not where others can see. What I feel for you is private."

She nodded, relief vying with regret. "Dinner's ready." She fought to steady her voice. "Are you hungry?"

"Starving."

She gestured toward the rug she'd spread a short distance from the fire. He recognized it instantly as the same one Jamil and Ali had wrapped her in. "Make yourself comfortable and I'll serve you."

Turning, she waved to someone occupying the next tent and Malik choked off a laugh. If he'd found the front of her caftan provocative, the back was even more so. It was totally sheer, one stray peacock feather seeming to float toward earth curling modestly across her buttocks. Or attempting to. The pert roundness couldn't quite be concealed by a single feather, a fact he quite appreciated.

A moment later a trio of musicians drifted closer. A *nay,* a *tablah* and a *qanun* provided the reed, percussion and strings for the music. Dancers gathered, swaying in time to the music, their movements nowhere near as seductive as Zara's. While he watched, Zara expertly removed the chicken from the spit and served him the various dishes she'd prepared. Then she took a seat at his side. He stripped the tenderest morsels from the bones of the chicken and fed them to her, selected the choicest bits of vegetable for her pleasure. His cup became hers, his honeyed dates best suited for her lips.

Her thanks came in the form of lingering kisses and heated glances that assured him he wasn't the only one eager for the night to progress. It wasn't until the last fig had been consumed and the final morsel of food enjoyed that he realized the dancers and musicians had faded away. He stared out at the campsite in surprise. At some point, the tents had been silently folded and the people had vanished as unexpectedly as they'd come. He'd been so preoccupied with Zara, he hadn't even noticed.

As though it were the signal she'd been waiting for, she rose to her feet and crossed to the tent. The fire burned through her caftan, licking across the pale expanse of her back. She parted the tent flap and glanced at him over her shoulder. Her eyes were dark and filled with feminine mystique. Then she vanished inside, only the singing of silvery bells lingering in the air.

Zara stood just inside the tent and fought to take a breath. For some strange reason, her lungs refused to cooperate. She'd been so certain she'd made the right decision when she'd switched places with Matana. Now, in the single heartbeat it took for the tent flap to fall closed behind her, she wasn't as certain. Unfortunately time was working against her. It wouldn't be much longer before Hakem or Kadar uncovered her deception, which meant she either went through with her plan or her stepfather would win.

She moved deeper into the tent, troubled by a nagging question she'd struggled all day to ignore. Was she still doing this for king and country? Somehow she doubted it. In the few short days she'd been with Malik, everything had changed. She'd changed. What occurred in this tent tonight wouldn't be for Hakem's sake, or even Rasha's. It would be for her own.

The tent flap rustled as Malik entered. He stood by the entrance, silently watchful. "You're afraid again, aren't you?" he said at last.

There was no point in denying it. "Yes." The word that escaped sounded thin and reedy and pride forced her to repeat it. "Yes, I'm afraid."

"Why?"

His question burned deep, igniting emotions she'd kept frozen for a full decade. She couldn't lie to him. Not now. Not about something so life-altering. "When I decided to come here," she confessed, "I wasn't looking forward to what this night would entail."

He didn't seem particularly surprised. "Were your previous experiences so unpleasant?"

"It's not that. It's…"

"It's the stories you heard about me."

He said it so matter-of-factly that denial proved impossible. "Yes." She turned to confront him, hoping he'd understand. "I grew up listening to tales of the Scourge of Rahman. Whispered horrors of how you'd killed a relative of Kadar ibn Abu Salman and fled the country in disgrace."

"And you believed them?"

"There was no one to defend you," she explained simply. "No one who knew your side of the story."

"Are you asking for my side?"

"No." It was now or never. Either she took a leap of faith and trusted him or she ended this here and now. "I don't need to hear your side."

"Why?"

There was only one answer to that. "Because I trust you."

He closed his eyes for a brief moment. When he opened them again, she saw a lightness about him that hadn't been there before. "Thank you."

"You're welcome."

He left the front of the tent and approached a small table holding a bowl and pitcher of water. His presence dominated the spacious interior, filling her with an odd sense of danger. He poured water into the bowl and washed his hands. Glancing at her, he said, "Now I have a question to ask you."

"Only one?"

"One to start with." Her sense of danger intensified. "How did you come to Hakem's attention? How were you chosen as my gift?"

"My stepfather brought me to the king." That was true enough. "By agreeing to come here as your birthday present, I had the opportunity to find my American relatives."

"So you said." He dried his hands on a small towel she'd put beside the pitcher. "But you also mentioned another reason. A private one. Will you tell me about it now?"

She couldn't drop her gaze, any more than she could lie to him. "By agreeing to do this, I'm protecting Rasha."

He stilled. "How?"

"My presence in Rahman was causing a..." She sought for as accurate a description as possible. "A political disruption. By removing me, the disruption is removed."

It didn't take him long to leap to the most obvious conclusion. "Which means that either Hakem wanted you or Kadar. Though why that would cause any sort of political disruption—'' Malik's eyes narrowed. "Kadar was going to use you as an excuse to cause trouble.''

"Yes.''

"How?'' he repeated, the word containing more of a bite this time.

Tension gripped her. "That doesn't matter now that I'm with you.''

Malik's mouth tightened. "Not good enough, Zara. If Kadar could use you to cause trouble, he can use another woman.''

"No other woman would do.''

"Because Hakem wouldn't have been attracted to anyone else?'' Malik shook his head. "Despite what Kadar might have told you, Hakem would not have wanted you. Despite your beauty, despite any attraction he might have felt, Hakem would have remained faithful to Rasha.''

"I suspect you're right. But leaving Rahman ensured it.''

She could see him analyzing her words, searching for the telltale omission. "That still doesn't explain why you're so unique. Why would Kadar have succeeded in disrupting the political stability by using you?''

"Because my stepfather is a powerful man who would protect his only daughter.'' She didn't dare say more. "I decided it was best to leave and ensure Kadar's plans would fail, rather than to stay and risk his succeeding.''

Malik relaxed ever so slightly. "So we're both political sacrifices.''

His comment roused her curiosity. "Is that what you were? A sacrifice?''

"What do you think?" He tossed the hand towel aside and slowly approached. He moved with the grace of an Arabian leopard, looking strangely at home in the silken lair she'd created. "You say you've been taught to believe I'm a murderer, but still you agreed to come here. You had to be aware of what would be expected of you. And still, you agreed to stay. Weren't you afraid?"

"I was when I first arrived."

"And since then?"

It was so simple, the answer crystal clear. "Since then I've had the chance to form my own opinion."

"Are you saying your opinion of me has changed?"

He stopped inches from her. She'd thought him intimidating in a business suit and tie. But dressed in traditional Rahman dress, he exuded a power beyond any she'd known. "You're still a threat," she whispered. "But it's not to my life."

Her answer amused him. "If not to your life, then what?" he questioned softly.

"I wasn't supposed to feel anything this night. But I do."

"Is it your heart I threaten? Is that it, Zara?"

She closed her eyes and allowed the truth to wash over her. "Yes."

It was a painful admission, one she'd have given anything to deny. Falling in love with Malik had never been part of the bargain. But at some point in the last three days, she'd stopped seeing the Scourge of Rahman and seen the true personality of the man.

He wasn't a murderer, but someone whose spirit had been nearly ripped from him. Kadar had done that. She didn't know how. Nor could she even begin to guess why Malik had ended up accepting the blame for having taken a life. She only knew—with every fiber of her being—that he was innocent of the charge. Perhaps that explained why she'd done everything in her power to heal the emotional wound he'd received all those years ago, to return a piece of Rahman to him and perhaps an element of peace.

Malik's hands settled on her shoulders, his grip personifying the man—warm, strong, yet with an underlying gentleness. "Why are you with me tonight, Zara?" he asked.

"I'm here because I want to be."

"Is it to resolve the political situation in Rahman?"

"No. Not anymore."

"You made a promise to stay with me tonight. Do you remember giving me your word?"

"I haven't forgotten."

"I'm releasing you from that promise." His hands dropped to his sides, giving added impact to his statement. "You don't have to stay. You weren't meant for me, not as a birthday gift. You also weren't meant to be a casualty of Kadar's ambitions. And that's what you'd become if I took advantage of you now."

"Malik—"

He stilled her words with a shake of his head. "I'll help you find your relatives. Kadar will still be thwarted and Rasha protected. You have my word."

"What if I choose to stay?" she asked unevenly.

"Then I won't let you go any time soon. I'll locate your family, if that's still your wish. But you'll stay with me." As though unable to resist, he cupped her face, his expression deadly serious. "Once I have you, I won't be able to let go. Choose carefully, Zara."

"There is no choice. You're the only one I want."

Fierce joy burned in his gaze. "You won't be sorry. I swear it."

"There's something I haven't told you." She nestled against his shoulder. His fingers slid to her nape and she sighed in pleasure as he massaged the tense muscles. "Actually there are a couple of things I haven't told you."

"Will they make any difference to what happens tonight?" His question rumbled against her ear. "Will it change how we feel?"

"I hope not."

"Would you rather wait until morning to talk about these matters?"

"One confession won't wait. Or at least, it won't be an issue by the time morning arrives. So I'd better tell you that one up-front."

"And the other?"

"The other will take a while to explain."

The irony of it all made her smile. After having worked so hard to avoid telling him who she was, now she found herself in the peculiar position of wanting absolute honesty between them. She'd kept her identity a secret for several reasons. Initially it had been out of fear, fear that Malik would use her to retaliate against her family. Then, it had been to ensure that her stepfather didn't discover what had become of her before she'd been thoroughly compromised.

But lately it had been because of Malik. She knew if he realized *why* she was willing to sleep with him— that it was for the sake of her king and country—pride would prevent him from going through with it. He wanted her on his terms, not as some sort of sacrificial lamb.

She peeked up at him. "Maybe we should wait to

talk about that one matter. I have the impression you'd rather not start a serious discussion right now."

A broad grin cut across his face. "That wouldn't be my first choice, no. Why don't you make whatever confession you must to get you through the night. The other discussion can wait until we're both in a more philosophical frame of mind."

"I wouldn't bother you about this first issue, except—"

"Except?"

"I don't want it to take you by surprise. In case I yell or something."

His fingers stilled. "Yell."

"Right. Having grown up with so many brothers, I've heard things."

"Zara, you're not making sense. What have you heard?"

Her hand fluttered through the air before coming to rest on his chest. The steady beat of his heart filled her palm, offering an unspoken reassurance. "Just *things*. My brothers often talked among themselves when they didn't realize I was listening. But I was and heard them discussing problems with fainting and yelling and crying. I'm pretty sure I won't do any of that. At least, my mother laughed when I mentioned it to her. I'm fairly certain crying won't be a concern since I hardly ever cry. And I've never in my life fainted. But that yelling part..."

"Zara?"

"Yes, Malik?"

"If you don't tell me what the *hell* you're talking about, I'll be forced to do some yelling of my own. And I'd rather not, tonight of all nights."

"I've never made love before. There. I said it." She

forced out a laugh, though it sounded a bit ragged, at best. "I guess I was making a big deal about nothing. Right?"

Silence.

"Malik? Am I right?"

"Are you telling me that Hakem sent me a virgin?"

To her relief, Malik sounded remarkably calm. "He might not have known."

"You didn't think to mention that fact to him?"

"I don't believe it ever came up."

"What about with Rasha?"

Zara tilted her head to one side as she thought about it. "No. I don't recall her mentioning it, either."

He released her, thrusting a hand through his hair. "What about *you* mentioning it to *them?*"

His voice had taken on an odd texture and she gave him an inquiring look. "You sound peculiar, Malik."

"Answer my question! Why didn't you tell someone?"

"Do you think I should have?"

"Yes!"

"I don't see why," she argued with devastating logic. "I wasn't planning on going to bed with either one of them, so I don't see how it would be any of their business. But since I am planning to make love to you, I thought you should know the truth."

"Thank you for that."

"You're welcome."

"That was sarcasm, Zara, in case you didn't notice."

"Was it? Gee, it must have gone right over my head," she retorted sweetly. Slipping the *ilagah* anchoring her veil, she tossed it aside in a discordant clatter of bells. The veil followed, fluttering to the carpet in a cloud of emerald-green. Fumbling with the back of her caftan, she released the hook at the neck and shrugged free of the garment. It slid off her shoulders and pooled at her feet with a soft swish of silk. "Shall we get on with this?"

If his expression was anything to go by, she'd shocked him into silence. Perhaps he needed further direction.

She spread her arms wide. "Take me. I'm yours."

CHAPTER SEVEN

MALIK didn't move to take her, let alone make her his, and Zara frowned. Clearly she was doing something wrong. Perhaps he needed further reassurance.

"I promise, I'll try my very best not to yell, cry or faint. Will that do?"

He made a choked sound and her frown deepened as she struggled to figure out what was wrong with him. Before she could do more than take a single step in his direction, a helpless chuckle ripped free, growing in volume until it filled the tent. Hot color raced along her cheekbones. He was laughing at her!

"What's so funny?" she demanded, thoroughly insulted.

"Let's get on with it?" he finally managed to explain. "Take me, I'm yours?"

She planted her hands on her hips. "Well, what do you want me to say?"

"Oh, I think that about covers it."

He came for her, moving with a swiftness that caught her by surprise. She shrieked as he swept her off her feet. "Malik! What are you doing?"

"Yelling already, my sweet?"

"Yes." Had that jittery little word come from her? "Yes, I'm yelling. I think it must be nerves."

"That wouldn't surprise me a bit." He feathered a kiss across her brow. "And just so you know, I prefer moans to yells."

"I'll see what I can do about that." She buried her head against his shoulder. "Malik?"

"What's wrong now?"

"I'm naked."

"So I noticed." His voice grew impossibly tender. "You won't mind for much longer."

"Promise?"

"You have my word on it." To her surprise he carried her out of the tent and set her down on the rug beside the fire. "Wait here."

She tucked her legs close to her chest and wrapped her arms around them. Her hair curtained her, cascading over her shoulders and back to pool on the carpet around her. It offered only the illusion of modesty, though why she'd need even that after ripping off all her clothes, defied logic.

Malik returned a moment later carrying an armful of pillows and lightweight blankets. "Cold?" he asked.

"Not cold. Nervous." It amused her that the confession came with such ease. How odd. Somehow, sharing her most intimate thoughts with Malik seemed perfectly natural. "I'm glad I arranged for everyone to leave earlier. This might have gotten a little awkward otherwise."

"I'm glad we have our privacy, too." His hand swept the air to indicate everything from the star-filled sky, to the breeze rustling through the trees, to the gentle wash of water against the sand. "What happens between us should take place out here, not hidden away in a tent. I want it to be perfect for you."

How could it be otherwise when he'd be the one making love to her? She took a deep breath, acknowledging the truth. She hadn't chosen this course for the sake of Rahman, even though it had started out that way. She'd dreamt of this night her entire life, dreamt of sharing it with the man she loved with all her heart. And that man was Malik. Whether she'd known him a single day, a month or a year, her commitment was absolute. She was that certain—which left her only one option.

Cowardice had no place here.

She rose to her feet, her hair lifted by an errant breeze. Her curtain of protection parted, tossed backward over her shoulders in a crimson cape, baring her to his gaze. He stood perfectly still, waiting to see what she'd do, his gaze as black as the velvety canopy above them. And like the night sky, stars glittered in his eyes, a symphony of welcoming light within the dark.

Words were pointless. Her actions would explain everything. She went to him, removing his *gutra* and *thobe* with silent efficiency. As the garments fell, she feathered kisses across his bared skin, each lingering caress expressing her innermost feelings. Her hands became her voice, speaking all the words locked inside, her touch whispering of her contentment and desire, of her need and her trust, of her deepest desires and greatest hopes. She gave with generous innocence, instinctively following the dictates of her heart.

She didn't realize how affected he was by her efforts until the muscles beneath her hand corded with a burgeoning tension. His breath quickened, underlying his desperate struggle for control, and understanding dawned. He was fighting to protect her from himself, came the shocking realization, to hold himself back from a taking that would be as desperate as it was violent. Her gaze drifted slowly upward to lock with his. The firelight flickered across his face, his bronzed features forged into steely lines of hunger.

"Tell me what you want," she whispered.

"You."

She suspected the single clipped word was all he could manage. "Then take me, Malik. Because it's what I want, too."

It was all the prompting he needed. Gathering the shreds of his self-control, he moved with slow assurance. Gentle. Knowing. Determined. Where before she'd been the one to give him pleasure, he made it his mission to bring her joy. He started with her face, worshiping the slant of her brow, the curve of her cheek, the sweep of her jaw. Nothing escaped his attention. Not the sensitive length of her neck, nor the taut slope of her shoulders nor the soft leanness of her arms. He reveled in all of her, making sure nothing missed his slow, thorough attention.

By the time he cupped her breasts and drove the peaks to furrowed ripeness, the breath burned in her lungs. His teeth scraped across the tips, while his tongue soothed. Thought had long gone, replaced by a fierce craving that throbbed to a thundering pulse beat. Somehow the raging campfire at her feet had slipped into her veins and pooled in the pit of her stomach, sinking deep in her loins. She fought to speak, but found even words beyond her.

And still he didn't stop.

Malik sank to his knees, holding her up with strong, capable hands. From breast to belly to the flare of her hip, he blessed every inch of her with openmouthed kisses and teasing caresses. His fingers danced to a primitive song, teaching her body how to move to his rhythm. She fought to remain standing, her muscles trembling beneath the effort.

And still he didn't stop.

His hands cupped the back of her thighs, steadying her. And then he touched her, the most intimate touch she'd ever known. She shuddered, her head falling forward, her hair tumbling over him in a vibrant waterfall. A silent scream locked in her throat and she folded, sinking into his waiting arms. He eased her onto the pillows and drank from her mouth, his gentleness at odds with the intensity gathering between them. She'd never in her entire life imagined love could be so unbridled, so violent and consuming. It built in waves, desperate and urgent. His touch became harder, driving, barely giving her a chance to catch her breath before propelling her toward the next escalating urge.

She needed him, now, just as she had in her dream. She lay beneath him, bared to him, open and wanting. His kiss reassured her, a balm in the mist of a relentless storm. But it wasn't enough. She lifted herself toward the completion he offered, silently pleading for his possession. Gathering her close, he took her, filled her, stretched her, easing the momentary pain with loving words of passion. With that, the storm descended. With each surging stroke he changed her. She became an indelible part of him, as he became part of her. In that moment she knew the bond he created between them was absolute.

And then she soared, swirling toward the stars like the burning embers of the fire at their feet. He joined her in that moment of ecstasy, his head thrown back, the muscles in his throat straining. She wrapped herself around him, holding him close. Slowly the tremors subsided and with their passing, tears slid down her cheeks. What a fool she'd been. Did Malik know how she'd be changed by their joining? Was that why he'd insisted on her committing to him before making love to her?

There could only be one explanation. He hadn't wanted her to feel trapped. He'd given her the choice to walk away beforehand, suspecting that afterward, that choice would no longer be hers.

"Why are you crying?" His voice came softly through the night, close to her ear.

"Because I didn't know. I didn't realize—"

He seemed to understand, even without the words. "And now that you do?"

"I want to stay, Malik."

"Stay?" She heard the smile in his voice. "There was never any question of that."

He lifted her in his arms and carried her toward the lake. She gasped as he lowered her into the frigid water. Even in the middle of July, the mountain runoff had a bite to it. Gently he washed her, stoking fires she'd have sworn had been banked. Finally she fled the water. Not that she got far. He caught her before she'd gone more than three steps, tumbling her to the sand. They came together again with the water lapping at their feet, the heat from their joining driving away the chill.

Afterward they retreated to the tent. Exhausted, they collapsed to the silk sheets in a tangle of arms and legs, her long, damp hair binding them tight together. And then they slept, replete.

For the first time in months, Zara's dreams brought her peace. Because in her heart, she knew she'd found her way home.

The bleating of goats woke Zara at first light. For a moment, she thought she was back home, visiting one of Kadar's Bedouin relatives. But then she remembered. Remembered the night she'd spent in Malik's arms, the passion...and the love.

The bleating drifted closer and a large bearded and horned head poked through the tent flap. Spying the jewel-bright silk coverings, the goat snared a pillow and ripped it to shreds. Zara leapt from the bedding with a shriek of outrage. Snatching up the caftan she'd worn the night before she threw it on and chased the goat out into the morning sunshine. The small herd milled around the campsite.

"It would seem you forgot one small detail in your plans last night."

She turned to find Malik brewing coffee over a fresh fire and eyed the animals with a touch of concern. "They were supposed to have been returned last night. What are they still doing here?"

"Making a mess." He frowned at the remains of the pillow. "And eating our tent for breakfast. There's a cell phone in my car. Why don't you call the owner and have them picked up before we leave."

"You left your phone in the car?" She pretended to be shocked. "How unusual."

"I had more important matters on my mind, matters I didn't want interrupted by an inopportune call."

"I see." She shoved a goat from her path and shook her head in disgust. "This wasn't how I'd planned to start our day, you know."

"I can take care of that." His gaze swept over her, hotter than the fire blazing at his feet. "I was going to start it by bringing you a cup of coffee."

Her laughter faded, replaced by a quickening of desire that burgeoned deep in the pit of her stomach and spread relentlessly outward. "And then?"

"And then I was going to make love to you again."

She flew into his arms and threaded her hands through his hair, kissing him with a passion that she'd never known until Malik had come into her life. "I seem to have gotten my priorities wrong."

He gazed tenderly down at her. "They seem right to me."

"Oh, no. You come first. Goats are a distant second from now on. I promise."

His soft chuckle filled her with joy, particularly the ease with which it came. If she did nothing else, she'd see to it that all his days were filled with laughter, that she replaced the darkness he'd suffered the past ten years with light.

"Forget the coffee," she urged. "You're all I need this morning."

"In that case…" He swung her into his arms and started for the tent. In the distance, the sound of an engine broke the morning quiet and he hesitated, gazing toward the road. "It would seem someone's remembered the goats, after all."

"About time," she grumbled. "Pretty soon there won't be anything left of our tent but shredded silk and canvas and the few odd tent poles."

Malik didn't reply, but simply continued to stare toward the road. Lowering her to her feet, he pulled aside the tent flap. "Wait inside."

"What is it? What's wrong?"

"Nothing, I hope. Just humor me and wait inside. And Zara?" He dropped a kiss on the tip of her nose. "Get dressed."

She didn't argue. If Malik sensed something wrong, she'd trust his instincts. Darting into the tent, she slipped off the caftan and snatched up the clothes she'd initially worn to the campsite. It only took a moment to pull on her underwear, followed by the tan skirt and plain white blouse she'd arrived in the day before. Next she slipped into the ankle-high kid boots Alice had purchased for her and then reached for her comb. She could hear the car engine drone closer and an inexplicable feeling of panic took hold. She couldn't explain her reaction. But the closer the car came, the more her fingers trembled.

The hair she was attempting to braid slipped from her grasp and giving it up as a lost cause, she crept toward the entrance of the tent. She heard the car skid to a halt and doors slam. The bleating of the goats covered up the initial shout of whomever had arrived, so she couldn't make out the words. But there was no mistaking the flood of Rahman curses that followed, nor the person issuing them.

Kadar.

"Where is she?" he demanded.

Zara didn't wait to hear more. She burst from the tent. A limo was standing alongside the campfire, doors ajar. Her stepfather slowly exited the vehicle. He wasn't alone. Her stepbrothers had already left the luxury car and ringed Malik, knives drawn. She ran toward them, shoving at broad backs and heavily muscled arms until she'd gained the center of the circle. She took up a stance in front of Malik. "Get away from him. He hasn't done anything wrong."

"I told you to wait in the tent." Malik grabbed her around the waist and thrust her behind him. "This has nothing to do with you."

"It has everything to do with me." She grabbed the back of his *thobe* and tugged urgently. "I have to explain. Please, Malik."

"Take your hands off my daughter, Haidar," her stepfather demanded. "Or I'll cut you down where you stand."

Malik stilled. "Your *daughter?*"

Zara didn't need to see Malik's face to observe his reaction. Tension shot up his spine and knotted the muscles across the width of his shoulders. His hands collapsed into fists and his breathing quickened, sounding ragged in the sudden silence.

"I guess I was wrong about you not having to face an army of my outraged brothers," she whispered. Closing her eyes, she rested her head against his back. "I'm sorry, Malik. This is all my fault. Please let me try to stop them before someone gets hurt."

"Not another word, Zara," he ordered in a gritty undertone. "Not one more damn word."

Kadar barked a command. Instantly her stepbrothers sheathed their knives and stepped clear. "You didn't know she was my daughter, did you?"

Malik shook his head. "Your stepdaughter, I assume?"

"Yes. But still the daughter of my heart. She was to have been Hakem's wife."

"Not anymore," Malik retorted. She shivered at the harshness of his tone. "She belongs to me now."

"That's not going to happen."

Kadar gestured to his sons. It took all five of them to restrain Malik while her stepfather snatched her into his arms and carried her, fighting all the way, toward the limo. "Please, no. Let me stay with him," she cried.

"Have you lost your mind?" He subdued her with ease. "Zara, have you no sense? He's the Scourge of Rahman."

"I don't care. I love him. Please, Father. I beg of you. Don't do this."

"Love?" His jaw worked. "You little fool. You were meant for a king. What is love compared to that?"

"Love is everything!"

"Not for long." He caught her chin in his hand and forced her to look at him, forced her to witness the truth of what he planned to say. "He murdered Jeb, Zara. Do you understand what I'm telling you? It's been kept from you long enough. It wasn't just a relative he killed. He took the life of your own brother."

She could only shake her head, struggling to deny her father's words. He didn't give her time to react. Signaling a silent message to her stepbrothers, he thrust her into the back seat of the limo. The unmistakable sounds of flesh striking flesh followed them inside. Fighting free of Kadar's hold, she scrambled to the window, staring in horror as one of her brothers—she couldn't see who—slammed his fist into Malik's jaw, dropping him to the sand. An instant later, he disappeared beneath a pile of swinging fists. Only Paz refused to participate. Whether it was out of respect for her or due to his own distaste for the ensuing brawl, she couldn't tell.

"Make them stop before they kill him!" she pleaded with her stepfather. "I'll go with you. I'll go willingly, but only if you tell them to stop."

Kadar hesitated, then gave an abrupt nod. He called to his sons, ordering them to return to the car. Obediently they backed away and piled into the limo. Her last view of Malik was as he slowly climbed to his feet, battered and bruised, his *thobe* ripped beyond recognition. His gaze locked with hers and what she saw there brought tears to her eyes.

All the good, all the healing she'd accomplished over the past three days had been for nothing. Bitter darkness blackened the brief lightness of his soul. Where once tenderness had glittered, revenge raged instead. She'd lied to him, even if by omission. She'd used him. Or so he thought.

And with that one look, she knew he intended to get even.

"She belongs to me and I want her back!"

"What an interesting way to greet your king," Hakem remarked dryly. "Please, Malik. Don't stand on ceremony. Come right in."

Malik strode into his cousin's quarters—rooms that had once been his father's. Rooms that would have been his, had his life followed a different path. To his surprise, that knowledge no longer had the power to infuriate him. Could time have truly healed those wounds? Or had one kindhearted, thoroughly irritating redhead—a redhead with sunny hazel eyes and far too many brothers—managed to exorcise the pain from his past?

"This is no longer my country, remember?" Malik thought to mention. "I was run out."

"As I recall, you chose to leave in order to prevent a coup and dropped all your problems and responsibilities on my doorstep while wallowing in the decadent lifestyle of your adopted country."

"Oh, that's right." Malik grinned. "I must have forgotten a few details over the past ten years."

Hakem stared for a full minute, his expression one of patent disbelief. Then he erupted from his chair. "It's good to see you smile, my friend." He wrapped his cousin in a fierce embrace. "I didn't think I'd ever see anything but pain or anger in your eyes. I am glad to discover I was wrong."

Malik suffered through a prolonged back pounding,

before he was finally released. "I'm serious, Hakem. I want Zara. And I don't intend to leave without her."

"She's not mine to give," Hakem offered apologetically. "Kadar has her. Rumor has it, he's furious."

"I don't doubt it. Is he likely to hurt her?"

Hakem shook his head. "She's his only daughter. He couldn't love her more if he'd been her natural father."

"Really? Then what was he doing giving her to you?"

Hakem pretended insult. "I'll have you know, any woman would be honored to take me as a husband."

"But only one woman will ever hold your heart," Malik retorted. "Zara deserves better than that."

"The decision isn't up to either of us. Her father controls her destiny now."

"We'll see." Frustration drove Malik to pace the generous width of the room. "Explain what happened. How did Zara become involved in all this political intrigue? Did you know she planned to take the place of the woman you were sending me? Did you arrange it?"

Hakem held up his hands to ward off the barrage of questions. "I had no idea or I'd have stopped her. Calm yourself, my friend. You're as jumpy as a sand cat. Come and sit. We'll share a cup or two of coffee and discuss the situation like two rational men."

Malik watched in mounting irritation as his cousin made a ceremony of pouring coffee from a tall silver *dallah*. If he wanted answers to his questions, he didn't have any choice but to do as his cousin requested and join him. Taking a seat, he accepted the dainty, handleless cup. The aromatic odor of cardamom mingled with the richness of the roasted beans and he inhaled, surprised to find his tension easing.

"Good, yes?" Hakem asked with a knowing smile.

Malik took an appreciative sip of the greenish-brown brew and nodded. "This is excellent. My thanks." It had been a long time since he'd taken his coffee in the traditional Arabic fashion or had it combined with the bitter spice. Too long.

"To answer your first question, Zara became embroiled in all this when Kadar hatched the plan of offering her to me as a second wife. It occurred shortly after the birth of my third daughter."

Malik settled against the cushions and took another sip, rolling the pungent brew across his tongue. "He hopes she'll give you the sons Rasha hasn't."

"That's what he's said."

"And what he's not saying is that he hopes his daughter's sons inherit the throne. It would give him more power than anyone could comfortably control."

"That's my guess, as well, especially when he pushed to have the wedding before Rasha gave birth."

Malik nodded in perfect understanding. "He was afraid your wife might produce a son, I assume, and give you an excuse for refusing Zara."

"Yes. Zara's solution was actually quite clever. By switching places with Matana, the woman chosen for your birthday present, she's prevented the wedding from going forward. Kadar's political ambitions have been undercut and since she's been living with you without benefit of a chaperon, I can honorably refuse her as my second wife."

"There's only one problem."

"You mean Zara's future, I assume."

Malik inclined his head. "That's why I've come. I intend to settle matters once and for all."

Hakem's laughter was empty of amusement. "Kadar

will never give her to you. His hatred hasn't lessened these past ten years.''

"I realize that. But I have a plan.''

"It must be some plan, my friend.''

"It is.'' Malik smiled, holding out his coffee cup. "First tell me how Rasha's doing and then I'll explain the part you'll play in my scheme.''

"I'm supposed to what?'' Zara asked her stepbrother in disbelief.

Paz grimaced. "I know. I don't understand it, either. But King Haidar has commanded your presence at the palace.''

"But…why?'' She paced the length of her bedroom. "This can't be good.''

"Father thinks it's either to get an explanation from you about what happened or…''

"Or *what?*'' She clasped her hands so tight her knuckles turned white. "Please, Paz. I can't stand any more.''

"Or to go ahead with the wedding,'' he admitted reluctantly.

Zara flinched. "No. I don't believe he'd ever agree to that. Not after—''

"Then it's true? You and…and the king's cousin were lovers?''

Even Paz refused to speak Malik's name aloud, she realized sadly. "Did you have any doubts?''

"I don't understand any of this, Zara. Have you lost all ability to tell right from wrong? Have you no sense of honor or duty to your family? What were you hoping to accomplish by giving yourself to that man?''

"I was hoping to prevent Kadar from forcing me into

a marriage that I didn't want," she retorted. "A marriage our king didn't want, either."

"You don't know that for certain."

She shot him a direct look. "Yes, Paz. I do." She ended the discussion with an impatient gesture. "Now tell me what happened with Jeb and why the truth was kept from me."

"Your mother insisted you not be told," Paz explained readily enough. "And Father went along with it."

"And the accident itself? What happened?"

Paz evaded her gaze. "It was a long time ago and I was small. I don't remember all the details."

Zara eyed him shrewdly. "You remember. Tell me. What happened?"

She didn't think he'd agree. But then he shrugged. Crossing to her window, he stared at the courtyard below. "It was Prince Malik's twentieth birthday. He and our brother Asim were best friends and he'd come to celebrate."

She clasped her hands together. "Something went horribly wrong, didn't it?"

Paz nodded. "They quarreled. Over what, I can't say. A woman, perhaps. Or more likely a political appointment. Whatever the argument, it was serious."

"And then?"

"The prince stormed out, swearing never to return. According to gossip, he was furious. Out of control. His parting words were a curse. He swore to bring down the house of Salman, son by son, if necessary."

"I don't understand. How is Jeb involved in this?"

"He was playing outside." Paz's voice dropped so low she had to struggle to hear. "They claim the prince ran him over. That he deliberately murdered Jeb as a warning that he'd do as he'd promised and destroy us all.''

"No!" Zara rushed to Paz's side and caught his arm. "That's a lie! Do you hear me? Malik would *never* do such a thing, never hurt an innocent child, no matter how angry he was."

"Jeb wasn't playing near the street," Paz replied tonelessly, shaking off her hold. "He was beneath a tree, well out of the way. When Father reached the scene, Malik's Jeep had Jeb pinned to the tree trunk and the prince was standing there, watching your brother die."

"There's some other explanation," she insisted. "There has to be."

"Enough!" Paz erupted unexpectedly. "I don't wish to discuss it further. And if you were wise, you wouldn't mention it to Father, either. It wouldn't take much to push him over the edge right now. Be smart for once. Beg his forgiveness and pray his anger dies soon."

Tears filled Zara's eyes. "It isn't Kadar's forgiveness I need. It's Malik's. I didn't tell him who I was and now he thinks I've used him."

Paz stared at her oddly. "You…you care for him?"

"I love him." The words came in a fierce undertone, passionate and unequivocal.

Paz shook his head, his expression horrified. "But, you can't. You can't love him. Father will never allow you to go with him, not after what happened. He'll never forgive the man who killed Jeb."

"Paz—"

He cut her off with a sweep of his hand. "You don't understand, Zara. Father's too powerful. Look at what he did to Malik. He brought down the future king of Rahman!"

"I stopped Kadar," Zara said softly. "Now King Haidar and Rasha are safe."

"You've only stopped Father if the king refuses to marry you. He might not, despite what happened between you and the Scourge. Who knows what pressure Father will bring to bear in order to force the marriage."

"Then I'll find another method to stop him. I won't marry Hakem. I won't."

Her stepbrother shook his head. "You might not have a choice," he said gently. "Kadar ibn Abu Salman always gets his way."

"Not last time." Zara set her chin. "And not this."

"You've caused quite a commotion."

"Yes, Sire," Zara replied. "I seem to excel at it."

Hakem opened the door to an enclosed atrium and glanced down at her. "It's a personality quirk best revealed before the wedding ceremony takes place, wouldn't you agree?"

Oh, no. Please let her have heard wrong. "Wedding ceremony?" she stalled. "You can't mean—"

"Did you doubt there'd be one?"

She'd wondered why he'd requested a private conversation. Now she had her answer, though not one she liked. "That was my goal," she answered with painful honesty. "Are you saying we're still to be married?"

He hesitated. "I haven't decided. Until I do, you'll remain at the palace."

She didn't understand why he found it necessary to keep her here. But then, it wasn't her place to question Hakem's decisions. "Kadar has agreed to this?"

"I'm his king. Of course, he's agreed."

"That would be a first," she murmured.

"It would only be a first if it didn't fit in with his own plans."

She couldn't help smiling over that. "I stand corrected."

One of the palace servants approached and murmured something in Hakem's ear. "Tell them I'll be right there." He turned to Zara. "My apologies. It would seem an urgent matter requires my attention. Take your time and explore. If I'm able, I'll join you later and we'll finish our discussion."

She fell back on formality. "Thank you, Sire. I look forward to it."

The atrium had been designed by Malik's mother as part greenhouse and part aviary and Zara was perfectly content to wander around on her own. It would come as a welcome relief after so many days spent confined to her room. Plants of every description flourished within the carefully modulated environment and birds of all types flitted from tree to bush.

The scents were particularly intoxicating and Zara took her time, stopping periodically to sniff an exotic flower or watch the ritualistic courtship of a pair of mating birds. Just as she'd decided to return to her room, footsteps sounded behind her. She turned, expecting to see the king.

She was wrong. It wasn't him and all she could do was stand and stare in disbelief.

"Hello, Zara," Malik said. He lifted an eyebrow at her expression, his amusement coldly derisive. "Why so surprised? Did you really think I'd ever let you go?"

CHAPTER EIGHT

ZARA shouldn't have been surprised to see Malik, but
somehow she was. She fought for control, aware that
her color ran too high and her heart beat too rapidly.
Did he notice? Considering how observant she'd found
him in the past, she didn't doubt it.

"What are you doing here, Malik?" *What took you
so long?*

"I've come for you."

Fear for his safety overrode every other concern.
"Does Hakem know you're here?"

"This is Hakem's home. Of course, he knows." He
stalked toward her. "Is that all you have to say, Zara?
Don't you want to offer any explanations? Defend yourself? Justify your actions?"

She hadn't been near him in a full week. And yet,
her memory of their last moments together continued to
haunt her. She saw him again, picking himself up from
the sand, bruised and battered, his hair tumbling across
his forehead, while vengeance darkened his eyes.

"What happened to the goats?"

His breath came in an exasperated rush. "After everything that's happened, that's all you can think to
say?"

"I can think of plenty to say." *How can I protect
you from Kadar's wrath? How will I live without you
when I'm forced to marry another? Please, take me in
your arms and steal me from this place.* She shrugged

134

carelessly in the hopes it would cover her distress. "The goats seemed the safest place to start."

"The owners arrived not long after you left."

"You mean, after I was dragged off," she retorted evenly.

He didn't argue the point. "Why didn't you tell me who you were?"

"You're a smart man, Malik. I shouldn't have to explain something so self-evident." A line of white scored his jawline and the corners of his mouth, evidence of how tightly he held himself in control, and she realized in that moment that he was bone-deep furious. Her flippant manner hadn't helped the situation and her breath escaped in a shaky sigh. "You came here to get even, didn't you?"

"It crossed my mind."

"There's nothing you can do to Kadar. He's too well protected."

"It's not Kadar I'm after."

She understood then and tension coiled in the pit of her stomach. What had transpired between them was personal. She'd violated his trust, broken a promise she'd sworn to keep. No. It wasn't Kadar he wanted to get his hands on. It was her.

"What would you have me say, Malik?" She gripped her hands together to hide their trembling. "I told you there were secrets I'd kept from you. If Kadar hadn't shown up when he had—"

"We would have made love again."

Her color deepened. "All right, fine. We would have made love again. But after that I would have informed you of my identity and explained why I'd been sent."

"You weren't *sent*. You chose to come to me. You chose to use me in order to thwart Kadar." He grasped her chin and lifted her face to his, examining her features one by one. "I should have realized who you were. All the clues were there."

"I don't look like Jeb or my mother. They were both blond and had the palest blue eyes I've ever seen."

"I remember," he said in a stark voice.

This wasn't the time nor place to go into the events surrounding her brother's death. "I'm not sure whom I take after," she said, hoping to draw his focus from the past.

To her relief, she succeeded. "But you offered enough information for me to make the connection. If I hadn't been so distracted, I'd have figured it out."

She didn't bother to ask what had distracted him. She'd done her best to ensure he remained off guard until she'd accomplished her goal. "Would you have objected if I'd told you who I was when I arrived?"

"You're damned right I would have objected!"

Her anger rose to match his. "I'd have thought you'd find it the perfect opportunity for revenge."

"Is that what you think of me? After all the time we spent together, after all we shared?" He thrust her away and paced deeper into the atrium, as though needing to put as much space between them as possible. "I'm still the Scourge of Rahman, aren't I?"

"No, of course not!" She went after him. "I realized almost right away that you weren't the man Paz described. It only took—"

Malik turned unexpectedly, absorbing the impact of her body as she tumbled into his arms. He used her momentum to gather her close. "It only took what, Zara?"

She closed her eyes, giving him the confession he craved. "It only took a single kiss." She reveled in the strength of his arms, the warmth of his hand, the unique scent of his body. It was paradise and torture all in one. "Revenge might have occurred to you. It's a natural reaction. But once we spent some time together, you would have changed your mind. You're not a vengeful man."

He filled his hands with her hair, tangling his fingers in the silken strands. "You've more confidence in my abilities than I have. If I'd known it was Kadar's daughter wrapped in that carpet, you wouldn't have been granted a three-day grace period. I promise you that."

"Make up your mind, Malik. Either you'd have taken me out of revenge or—" For some reason she couldn't bring herself to offer any other possibility. Certainly not the one she'd assumed when he'd carried her to the fire and made love to her with such tenderness. Nor when he'd bathed her in the lake beneath a star-filled sky or joined with her on the water's edge with the chilly waves doing little to cool the burning heat that drove them together. "My point is, regardless of our initial motives in coming together, the result would have remained the same. You and I would still have become lovers."

"That's where you're wrong. You're forgetting one small detail. You were promised to Hakem. I wouldn't have taken what belonged to him, not even to exact a little revenge on Kadar."

His comment infuriated her. "I don't belong to the king. I don't *belong* to anyone. Not Kadar. Not Hakem. And especially, not you."

"That's not what you said a few nights ago. You gave yourself to me. And when you did, you made a promise." He lowered his head, his mouth feathering a path along her jawline to the pulse beneath her ear. "Or have you forgotten that, too?"

Pain ripped through her, amplified by his touch. Want fought with discretion, a decidedly uneven match. "I haven't forgotten a single moment of that night." She struck out in despair. "Have you?"

His breath exploded from his lungs, hot against the side of her neck. She could feel his pride and anger vie with the sweet memories of their time together. "How could I?" he whispered. "How could I forget?"

"Then hold on to that night, Malik. Believe in it," she pleaded. "I didn't expect Kadar to come for me. I thought he'd disown me when he found out what I'd done."

Malik remained silent for a long moment, holding her close while the tension slowly drained from his body. "How angry was he?"

"I've never seen him so crazed."

She shuddered. If it hadn't been for Paz's interference, she might have gotten her wish and been disowned on the spot. But Kadar had always held as soft a spot for his youngest son as for her.

Her shiver didn't escape Malik's notice. He pulled back to examine her, as though searching for signs of abuse. "Did he hurt you?" he demanded roughly.

"He'd never hurt me, Malik. But what he did to you..." She lifted a trembling hand to his face. The faintest shadow of a bruise still marred his cheekbone and a nearly healed cut curled from the corner of his mouth. "I'm so sorry."

"I recovered. Faster than if you hadn't ended the fight."

"You heard?"

"Heard you tell Kadar you'd leave willingly if they'd stop? Yes."

"And he did make them stop. For all his faults, my stepfather loves me. He was..." She swallowed hard. "Once he got past his anger, he was disappointed."

"Because he wanted you married to a king."

"That was one reason."

"Perhaps he should have considered that option before forcing me out of the country. If he'd bothered to show you to me, we could have reached a settlement. You might have been little more than a child, but I'd have waited for you."

It took her a moment to understand what he meant. "Are you saying you would have wanted me even if you'd become king?"

His jet-dark eyes provided the answer before he uttered a single word. "How can you doubt it? Once I saw you, you would have been mine, whether I was the King of Rahman or plain Malik Haidar, financier."

She fought against the unexpected bite of tears. "So I was destined to become your mistress or a second wife, no matter which path our futures took."

"I didn't make you my mistress." His tone had turned impossibly hard. "You put yourself in my bed."

"And you know why I did."

His expression closed over, more distant and remote than ever before. "I know. I know you came to me in order to avoid marriage to Hakem."

"And to prevent Kadar from gaining a political advantage through that marriage."

"I also know that any man would have solved your problem."

She stared, appalled. "What are you saying?"

"I'm saying that you were intent on being compromised and you didn't particularly care who did it, so long as the deed was done."

The fact that he spoke the truth only hurt all the more. "You're right. When I came up with the plan, I didn't give any thought to who would—" Her voice broke and she fought to firm it, with only limited success. "Who would compromise me. It didn't matter, so long as I was no longer an acceptable wife for Hakem, and Kadar's political ambitions were stymied."

He stepped away from her. "So you used me."

"Yes. And I expected to hate it as much as I expected to hate myself," she retorted passionately. "But that's not what happened. I expected to give myself to the Scourge of Rahman. And instead—"

"Instead?" he prompted, his gaze watchful.

She closed her eyes. "What difference does it make? You're right. It didn't matter who I slept with. It accomplished the same goal in the end. I should feel ashamed of the choice I made." She looked at him then. "If it had been any other man, I would have been ashamed. Bitterly ashamed."

"But not with me."

"No," she whispered.

She sensed a softening in him, though it didn't show in his expression or ease the harshness of his voice. "And why was it different with me?"

"You want it all, don't you, Malik?"

"Every bit."

She shook her head, refusing to give him the satisfaction. "That's unfortunate, because you're not getting any more from me. I've said too much already."

"Explain."

"Haven't you heard? Hakem might still marry me. If I took this any further, it would dishonor him and I

refuse to do that. I've offended him enough already."
To her surprise, Malik gave an understanding nod. She
approached and touched his arm. "There's one more
fact you should know."

"More secrets?"

"Not a secret. Just something you should think
about." She'd caught his attention with that one. "I
didn't have to sleep with you, Malik. Living under your
roof for three days and nights was more than enough to
give Hakem the out he needed. He could claim I wasn't
acceptable to have as his wife and not even Kadar
would have argued the point. Even if you swore you
hadn't touched me, no one would have believed you.
And Hakem would still have had his excuse."

Malik cupped her neck and urged her against him.
"There's something you should think about, too.
Something you might mention to Hakem before you
agree to marry him."

"And what's that?"

Lowering his head, he took her mouth in a slow, thorough kiss. Every instinct she possessed screamed for
her to resist, but her heart had control of her body. She
slid her arms around Malik's waist and clung to the
back of his *thobe,* her lips parting beneath the urgent
pressure of his. His tongue eased home and she greeted
the caress with a soft moan of welcome. How could she
marry Hakem when more than anything she wanted to
return to the campsite in the middle of a Californian
valley? To spend a lifetime in Malik's arms, experiencing endless nights like the one they'd shared on his
birthday.

He locked her hips against his, forcing her to ac-
knowledge that his desire ran as hot and fierce as hers.
"You see how it is between us? Nothing has changed."

"Everything has changed. I'm not available to you. Not anymore."

"Are you sure? If I came to you in the middle of the night, slipped into your bed with no one the wiser, would you turn me away?"

"Don't!" She lowered her voice, pleading. "Hakem will forgive you much. I can see how he loves you. But he'd never forgive such an insult. Please, don't take that sort of risk. Not for me."

He laughed. "Why do you think I'm here, if not for you?"

One of them had to be sensible. She pulled free of his arms and took a quick step away. "You have to go. Please, Malik. I don't want anything to happen to you. If someone were to see us together—"

To her relief, he gave in with an understanding nod. "I'll leave for now. But I'll be back." He started to walk toward the exit, before stopping abruptly and spinning in his tracks. "That small detail I mentioned...? The one you might want to warn Hakem about?"

"What is it?" she asked impatiently.

"You could be carrying my child. Tell him that, will you?"

"Did you know Malik was here?" Zara asked Rasha.

"I knew."

"Am I the last to find out?"

Mischief gleamed in Rasha's light brown eyes. "I believe Hakem's hoping your stepfather will be the last."

"I can't argue with that." Zara sank onto the couch next to Rasha. "Why didn't you tell me he was here?"

"Hakem warned me not to." She grimaced, shifting in a vain attempt to make herself more comfortable.

"You couldn't have been too surprised to see him, though."

After that final glare he gave at the campsite? "No. I had the feeling he'd want to even the score between us."

"Even the score?" Rasha looked intrigued. "What did you do to him?"

"It's what I didn't do. I neglected to tell him who I was. I'd promised to remain with him." Zara shivered. "He wasn't happy when I broke my word. And he was even less happy to discover that my stepfather was the man who'd ruined his life."

"Is that what Malik said? That his life was ruined?"

"Not in those exact words. But there's a lot of bitterness." She'd hoped to leave him less bitter. Perhaps she'd have succeeded if Kadar hadn't arrived at such an inopportune moment. "If not for Kadar, Malik would have been king."

"And instead of the responsibilities that come with that position—the turmoil, the political strife and intrigue, the lack of a personal life, the inherent danger from outside oppositions—Malik has the freedom to do whatever he wants. He runs a multimillion dollar company, is highly respected in the business community and can come and go wherever and whenever he chooses."

"He can come and go...except to Rahman."

Rasha struggled to her feet and Zara hastened to give her a hand. "Who told you that? It's not true at all."

"I assumed—"

"Malik wasn't banished," Rasha explained. "He left of his own choice in order to make the transition easier for Hakem."

"Then... He hasn't come back for me?"

"I have no idea. You'll have to ask Malik that."

"Ask Malik what?" Hakem interrupted from the doorway.

Rasha held out her hands to her husband. "Zara was wondering why your cousin has returned."

"This is his homeland. What other reason does he need?" Hakem glanced at Zara. "You saw him in the palace, I assume?"

A blush warmed her cheeks. "We...we spoke."

The king lifted an eyebrow. "No doubt he wanted to offer his congratulations on your impending marriage."

Zara stared at him, stricken. "Then you've decided?"

"I've decided you're to marry. The choice of bridegroom is still under consideration."

He dismissed the subject by lifting Rasha in his arms and carrying her back to the couch. "You know what the doctor has said. You mustn't tax yourself, my jewel." He lowered her gently to the cushions. Kneeling at her side, he spread his hand across her extended belly and caressed his child through the thin layer of silk she wore. Rasha leaned forward and threaded her fingers through his hair.

"This one's impatient to join us," she murmured.

"Yes, I can feel the restlessness. But a few days wait would be more convenient."

She laughed, the sound filled with warm humor. "I always endeavor to please my king. I'll see what I can do."

His laughter linked with hers, and then he gathered her close and kissed her. Zara shut her eyes, her pain beyond words. Silently she slipped from the room. She'd known that sort of adoration for one brief night before it was taken from her. Malik had held her like that, had whispered tender words of love to her, had touched her with a similar passion. How could she allow another man to put his hands on her after what she'd shared with him? The answer was simple.

She couldn't.

What in the world did she do now? She couldn't marry Hakem, any more than Kadar would allow her to marry Malik—assuming such an offer were made. Her fingers splayed across her abdomen. And what if she carried his child? What if that one sweet night had borne fruit? She had to explain the situation to Hakem, make it clear to him—

As though her thoughts had summoned him, Hakem's voice came to her. "Zara? Are you all right?"

She hastened to wipe the dampness from her cheeks before turning to face him. "I'm fine. Does Rasha need me?"

"She's resting, which gives me the opportunity to speak to you alone. I wanted to ask a favor."

"Anything."

"Keep an eye on her. She tries to protect me from matters she deems unimportant." His mouth twisted. "As far as I'm concerned, nothing about her current condition is unimportant. You're to inform me if her situation changes."

"Yes, Sire." She hesitated. "We never finished our conversation in the atrium."

"There's something more you wish to say?"

She moistened her lips. "Did Kadar explain… everything? About Malik and…and what happened between us?"

"What are you trying to tell me, Zara?"

She could see she'd have to be blunt and take the consequences, whatever they might be. "Malik and I were lovers."

"I assumed as much."

"There's one other detail. Malik reminded me—" Her voice broke and she fought for control. "I could be pregnant from that encounter."

"I assumed that might be a possibility, as well."

Had his voice gentled? She couldn't be certain. "I wanted to be positive you had all the facts before making your decision about a marriage. I wasn't sure Kadar had been totally frank with you."

"So you've taken that task on yourself." He tilted his head to one side. "I can't help wondering why?"

He reminded her of Malik in that moment, his gaze every bit as intense, his expression demanding, his tone imperious. Only absolute honesty would do, given the circumstances. "It's my responsibility to tell you the truth. And the truth is... I gave myself to Malik of my own free will."

"To prevent our marriage?"

"That was the initial plan. But then—"

"Then?"

She gave him a frank look. "I love Malik, Sire. And after watching you and Rasha together I realized that to share with another man what I shared with Malik would be impossible."

Hakem shrugged. "I already have love. I wouldn't expect that from you. Your purpose would be to ensure an end to political strife."

She flinched. What a fool she'd been to think her feelings mattered. Kadar had already proven they didn't. She lowered her gaze, hoping to hide her distress. "I see."

"There is another matter we need to discuss, on a different topic altogether." He folded his hands behind his back. "Malik has made a request."

"A request, Sire?"

"He feels under an obligation to you. Apparently you gave him something for his birthday, something he's unable to return. As a result, he wishes to balance the scales between you, so neither of you are under any further obligation. I have agreed."

She shook her head in bewilderment. "I don't understand."

"He's asked my permission to present a number of gifts to you. It's a reasonable request. So, for the next three days, you will be gracious enough to accept these gifts, whatever they might be. At the end of that time, all debts will be satisfied and this matter concluded. Do I make myself clear?"

It didn't take much effort to read between the lines and his pronouncement devastated her. She would have three days with Malik. Three days to settle their relationship. After that, their time together would end. It was the same number of days she'd had with him in California. She doubted it was a coincidence and the irony bit deep. "Yes, Sire," she murmured. "I'll do as you've requested."

And she'd keep her word. But how would she survive afterward?

"Pardon, my lady." The maid roused Zara from an exhausted slumber. "Prince Haidar requests your presence."

"Malik? Malik wants me?"

"Yes, my lady."

Zara hastened from the bed. "Please let him know I'll be with him as soon as I've dressed."

She didn't waste any time. Her king had requested that she graciously accept whatever gifts Malik had prepared and that's what she'd do. Could she help it if she'd take pleasure in the command? Excitement trembled through her. What sort of gifts could he have gotten for her? There was nothing she'd ever asked of him, nothing she needed or wanted. Except…

Except for Malik, himself.

Unable to explain her actions, she chose one of the outfits he'd purchased for her—the ivory skirt and Victorian lace blouse. She'd been amazed to discover them waiting in the closet when she'd returned to the palace. Now she understood how it had happened. Piling her hair in a loose knot on top of her head, she crossed to the music box that had belonged to Malik's mother. Opening the lid, she allowed the melody to wash over her, drawing strength and hope from the tender lullaby.

Maybe her situation would work out, after all.

Exiting the room, she was directed to Malik's quarters in the guest wing of the palace. She glanced hesitantly at the servant who escorted her to his rooms. "Are you certain…?"

"Royal permission has been granted," she was assured.

But whose royal permission? Malik's or Hakem's? She stepped into the room and stopped, staring in confusion. She'd walked into a bedroom suite. A huge four-poster canopied bed occupied one end of the room, while a fire crackled in a hearth at the other.

"What do you think?" Malik asked, appearing at her side.

"There's a fire," she marveled. "It's the middle of July and you have air conditioning blasting from the vents trying to keep this place cool and a fire in the fireplace."

"Ah, but there's a method to my madness." He held out a rectangular gift box. "This is for you."

A wave of shyness caught her off guard. She'd made love to this man, had even stripped naked in front of him. And yet, a simple present had her blushing like an awkward teenager. "Hakem mentioned you had a gift for me. I assume this is it?"

"It's part of my gift. My first gift," Malik clarified. "You understand that for the next three days, you're to come when I request it?"

"I understand." She looked at him uncertainly. "Did you choose three days because that's the same amount of time we spent together in California?"

"Yes."

She glanced at the box. "And this?"

"You're not dressed appropriately for what I have in mind. What's in the box will correct that." He inclined his head toward a door leading to the bathroom. "You can change in there."

"Malik—"

He folded his arms across his chest. "Are you questioning Hakem's orders?" he asked impatiently.

"No, of course not."

His voice hardened. "Then what are you waiting for? Go change."

She crossed to the luxurious bathroom without another word. *Gracious,* she reminded herself. She'd been ordered to be gracious and that's what she'd do, even if it killed her.

As soon as she'd closeted herself inside the bathroom, she pulled off the box lid, unable to contain her curiosity. Inside she discovered a short-sleeved cotton shift with a giant cartoon mouse decorating the front. She sank onto the edge of the dressing table chair and stared in utter bewilderment. She was supposed to wear *this?* What in the world could he have in mind that would make such an outfit appropriate to wear? Mystified, she searched through the box to see if she'd overlooked any other pieces of apparel. She hadn't.

It took five full minutes of debate before giving in to the inevitable. Removing her clothing, she donned the odd-looking shift. Then she opened the bathroom door and reluctantly returned to the bedroom.

Malik had changed, too. He was bare to the waist, his only covering a pair of drawstring cotton trousers. "Get in bed," he instructed.

Balking at this latest order, she crossed her arms beneath her breasts and shook her head. "I can't believe for one minute that Hakem agreed to such a thing. It's not proper."

His laugh held an ironic edge. "It's a little late to worry about what's proper, don't you think?"

One short week ago, she'd have run into his arms, eager for what he had in mind. But so much had changed since then. To her horror, tears pricked her eyes. "Please, Malik," she whispered. "Don't do this."

But he didn't relent. "Get in the bed, Zara. Now."

CHAPTER NINE

ZARA didn't dare argue when Malik used that tone of voice. She could only pray Hakem didn't hear of this latest indiscretion. Or Kadar! She shivered to think what her stepfather would do if he ever discovered she'd shared a bed with Malik again. Climbing into the four-poster, she slipped beneath the sheet and comforter, pulling them up to her neck.

"Now what?" she asked.

"Don't you know?"

Zara closed her eyes, torn between longing and dread. More than anything, she longed to be in Malik's arms. But this wasn't right. Not here. Not now. Not until Hakem had released her.

"What do you want from me?" she whispered.

"I don't want anything. I'm here to give you something, remember?"

He followed her into the bed, stealing away most of the spaciousness. Thumping the half dozen pillows into shape, he leaned back, making himself comfortable. No sooner had he settled into place, than the bedroom door opened. With a shriek of alarm, Zara pulled the covers over her head.

"Your breakfast," she heard someone say.

"Put it on the end of the bed, thanks," Malik replied. A moment later the bedroom door opened and closed again. "It's safe now. You can come out."

Zara cringed at the amusement threading his voice.

Gathering her nerve, she peeked from beneath the covers. "Did they see me?"

"She. And yes, she saw you. Or at least she saw your hair. Maybe if you'd left it down, it would have remained hidden. But I'm afraid this was sticking out." He flicked the knot on top of her head. The clip came loose and her hair showered down around her shoulders. "It's a rather distinctive shade, wouldn't you say? Not quite red and not quite blond."

Was she hyperventilating? It was either her or the mouse decorating the front of her shift. She pressed a hand to her heart. Maybe it was both of them. "I can't believe Hakem knew what you intended when he granted permission for these gifts. He's going to kill us when he finds out what we've been up to. And if he doesn't, Kadar will."

"Hakem isn't going to kill us. And the only way Kadar will find out is if you tell him." Malik cocked his head to one side. "You're not planning to tell him, are you?"

"*No!*"

"In that case, relax and enjoy my presents."

"This..." She gestured to indicate the fire and the bed. "This is a *present?* I've heard it called a lot of things, but not that."

"The present is down there." He pointed to the foot of the bed.

She stared blankly. "A tray of food and a newspaper?"

"Not any tray of food. And not any paper." He retrieved both. "I'll have you know this is the Sunday edition of an honest-to-goodness American newspaper. And the food is Sunday brunch. Have you ever had Sunday brunch before?"

"No."

He wrapped an arm around her waist and pulled her from beneath the covers. "Come. Lean back next to me." He adjusted the pillows. "How's that?"

"Fine," she replied cautiously.

"If you've never had Sunday brunch, then you don't know what you're missing. Sundays are very important days in America."

"They are?"

"Vital." He removed a napkin from the tray and spread it across her lap. His fingers brushed her thigh through the thin cotton of her shift, branding her with warmth. "They have a wonderful law there about Sundays."

She swallowed, struggling to focus on the conversation instead of on her reaction to his touch. "A law?"

"Right. It says that couples are required to spend at least one Sunday a month in bed, reading a newspaper while eating a late breakfast."

Her lips twitched. "Is that true?"

His expression fell into imperious lines. "Would I lie?" He removed the cover from one of the plates. "Let's see what we have here... Pancakes and maple syrup. Mixed fruit on the side. It doesn't get any better than that."

A wave of longing caught her by surprise. "I don't remember ever having pancakes."

He glanced at her, his gaze unexpectedly gentle. "Somehow, I didn't think so."

"And the newspaper?" she asked unevenly. "What's the significance of that?"

"Ah. Now that's as much fun as the pancakes. While we eat, we take turns reading to each other. Particularly the funnies."

"Funnies?"

"The comic strip. You'll love it."

He picked up the pitcher of syrup and upended it over her pancakes. Cutting a wedge off the stack, he fed her a bite. "Like it?"

She sighed in pleasure. "It's delicious."

"Almost as good as your *kibbe* and baklava."

While her fear eased, a different sort of tension built—the sort of tension that could only be the result of sharing a bed with a half-naked man. It left behind a distressing feeling of vulnerability, an utterly feminine reaction to a potent masculine threat. Desperation had her breaking into speech. "Why are you doing this, Malik? Is it because I fixed you a traditional Rahman meal, so you're fixing me a traditional American one? Is that how you plan to balance the scales between us?"

"Have it all figured out, do you?"

He flipped open the newspaper and her gaze shifted to the play of muscles across his shoulders and chest. She'd caressed those shoulders and kissed every inch of his chest. She squirmed, wishing he'd arranged for a larger bed. This one was shrinking by the minute.

"Which section would you like? Sports? Business?"

She allowed the conversation to shift into more neutral territory—*safer* territory, hoping her indiscreet thoughts would follow. "I'll take the front page."

"Don't forget you have to read me any interesting articles you come across."

She scanned the headlines. "In that case, we may be here most of the day. It all looks fascinating."

He offered her another bite of pancakes. "Then we'll be here most of the day." He shocked her by following up the pancakes with a lingering kiss flavored with an irresistible combination of hunger and maple syrup. "Shall I tell you about the other Sunday tradition?"

She shivered beneath the onslaught of desire. "Does it go with the newspaper and breakfast?"

"It comes after, my sweet. And it's slow and thorough and guaranteed to satisfy." His words were filled with passionate certainty, staking a claim she couldn't refute. "You have my word on it."

"We can't, Malik," she whispered miserably. "You know we can't."

"But we will. If not today, then soon." The certainty in his eyes terrified her. "You have my word on that, too."

Malik didn't send for her again until after dinner the next day. By the time the maid arrived, Zara's nerves were stretched taut wondering what he planned as his next "gift." Was that how Malik had reacted to her surprises? It joined them in some odd way, tying her to him more firmly than ever.

"Did he say how I was to dress?"

"He mentioned the clothes you wore yesterday would be appropriate."

Or rather, the ones she *hadn't* worn yesterday, Zara thought dryly. Dressing once more in the lace blouse and silk skirt, she wore her hair up, wondering if she did it to provoke him or so he'd take it down again.

Malik must have had a similar idea because he glanced at her hairstyle and grinned. "It won't last long," he announced, folding his arms across his chest.

"At least wait until we're alone." She hesitated. "Will we be alone?"

"Yes and no."

"That clarifies matters. Will we be leaving the palace?"

"The palace, yes. The grounds, no."

"Should I wear my veil?"

"You won't need a veil or *abaaya* for the next few days."

She gave up asking questions, willing to wait and see what he'd planned. Leading the way outside, Malik helped her into a white Lexus and drove around the compound to the far back where a wall separated the palace grounds from the encroaching desert. Moonlight poured down, gilding the landscape in silver, and night sounds stroked the air. Just over the wall, the wind whispered to the desert and the sand rustled in reply. In the far distance, a tufted sand cat screamed at the loss of his prey, no doubt a desert hare.

As soon as they reached the far corner of the compound, Malik slowed. Up ahead she could see a dozen Jeeps parked at intervals, facing a high section of wall. She stared in bewilderment. Malik pulled his car in among them, easing into an open section in front of the other vehicles. Though they were surrounded by others, they were also quite alone in the darkness.

"What now?" Zara whispered.

"Now we wait."

She remained rigid in her seat and gazed at the wall through the front windshield. She'd thought yesterday's experience odd. But sitting and watching an expanse of white plaster in the middle of the night had to be the strangest gift she'd ever received. How in the world did this even the scales between them? Suddenly a light illuminated the wall and music blared from hidden speakers. A man approached the car window and she jumped at his unexpected appearance. Bowing, he offered a tray to Malik.

"More pancakes?" Zara joked nervously.

"Nope. For a movie only popcorn and sodas will do."

"A *movie?*" She stared at the light playing across the wall. "We're going to watch a movie out here?"

"It's called a drive-in. It's another American tradition."

"You're joking." She couldn't get over it. "People really watch movies outside?"

"They go, but they don't watch much of the movie. The show is just an excuse."

"For what?"

He shot her a suggestive look. "Can't you guess?"

Her eyes widened. "You can't mean—"

"I do mean." He passed her one of the drinks. "It's the perfect excuse to eat popcorn and drink soda."

She chuckled. "Of course. That's exactly what I thought you were going to say."

The movie was a romance and she didn't object when Malik pulled her close. She nestled her head into the crook of his shoulder and fought hard not to cry. His gifts were becoming more and more difficult to handle dispassionately. They meant so much to her, in ways she found difficult to express. Had he felt the same about her gifts? Where once she'd given to him, wanting to return a piece of Rahman to his heart, now he gave what she'd never had before. Her roots. The flavor of her homeland. And most important of all, a missing piece of herself.

Zara glanced at him from beneath her lashes, studying the proud tilt of his head and striking arrangement of flesh on bone. Warmth curled in the pit of her stom-

ach. There wouldn't be many more occasions to spend
together. This was the second of their three days. Their
time was draining away with frightening speed, which
meant she should make the most of what little remained.
One question in particular troubled her, a question they
needed to address. She drew his attention by spreading
her fingers across his chest.

"What's wrong?" he asked, immediately sensing the
change in her mood.

"Will you tell me about Jeb?"

Tension rippled through him, gathering beneath her
hand. "Tell you what?"

"Until a couple of days ago, I'd assumed Jeb had
died in a car crash."

"And now?"

"Paz has given me a different story," she answered
readily enough. "He says you were in a rage because
of an argument with Asim. That you threatened to bring
down the house of Salman, son by son, if necessary.
And that you hit Jeb with your car in order to prove
you intended to fulfill your threats."

"Are you asking me to defend myself?" The emotion had been wiped clean from his voice, but the
bunching of muscles beneath her hand told a far different story. They warned of a man balanced on the edge
between fury and control. "You want to hear my side
of the story so you can judge for yourself who's telling
the truth?"

Was that what she was asking? She thought about it.
If their positions were reversed, how would she react if
Malik demanded she account for herself? Her mouth
pulled to one side. She'd be incensed. As difficult as it
would be, she'd want him to trust her despite all the
evidence to the contrary. It boiled down to one simple

fact: Did she believe in his integrity or didn't she? Was the man she loved a murderer without honor or conscience as Paz had claimed?

It didn't take any consideration at all.

"No," she replied gently. "I don't expect you to defend yourself."

Instantly the tension seeped away. "Thank you."

"Explain something else, instead. How did Kadar force you to abdicate?"

"That question I will answer." He took a moment to collect his thoughts. "You have to remember I'd just turned twenty, and my father was very ill. If he'd been stronger, events wouldn't have progressed as they had. He died the same week as your brother. Within days of his death, Kadar managed to convince the ruling families that I was without honor and not fit to take my father's place." The anger had fled and his words were offered with matter-of-fact precision. Even the tone held little expression. But the slight to his name must have cut deep.

"Oh, Malik. Did no one stand up for you?"

"Hakem did. And a few of the older princes who feared Kadar's ambition."

"How did your cousin become king?"

"I offered to abdicate if Kadar accepted Hakem in my stead. I knew he was strong and honorable and would rule well. I also knew that Kadar was bound to protect my cousin."

"Why?"

"He'd once saved the life of Kadar's youngest son, Paz. It gave Hakem a certain indemnity."

"A life for a life."

Malik inclined his head. "Kadar and Hakem agreed to my proposal and I relinquished the throne to begin my life again elsewhere. It's been a full life in many ways, but empty in others.'' The light from the screen flickered across his face, catching in the darkness of his eyes and throwing his features into stark relief. ''And then you came to me.''

''Came and left,'' she acknowledged regretfully. Awareness shivered through her. ''I shouldn't be here with you now. Not like this.''

''There's nowhere else you should be.'' He reached for her, loosening her hair so it pooled around her shoulders. ''You belong with me.''

''Belong?''

''Yes, belong. Though you'll notice I said *with*, not *to* me.''

She attempted a smile. ''That's a change. I seem to recall your claiming I was yours on more than one occasion.''

''You are.'' He cupped her chin and tilted her face to his. ''And before you start arguing, it goes both ways. I'm yours as much as you're mine. You must know that by now.''

Her mouth trembled. ''It doesn't matter what I think or what I know.''

''Of course it matters.'' He lowered his head and kissed her, tasting the softness of her lips. She clung to him, returning the embrace with a desperation underscored by despair. When the kiss ended, he traced his thumb along the fullness of her lower lip. ''Tell me *that* doesn't matter.''

''You have to stop. Someone might see.''

He simply smiled. ''No one will.''

''What…?'' She swiveled, looking toward where the other vehicles had been parked.

They were gone.

"Problem?" Malik asked blandly.

"We're alone. Again."

He grinned at her suspicious tone. "Hakem trusts me."

"Then Hakem must be—" To his amusement, she broke off self-consciously. "Anything I might say as far as that's concerned is likely to get me beheaded," she muttered.

"Oh, we don't behead people anymore. He might chop off your hair, but you won't lose your head."

"My hair!"

"That or confine you to my quarters for an indefinite period."

Her sigh shivered between them. "That wouldn't be much of a punishment. In fact, it would be a delight."

Her honesty pleased him. "I'd make sure of it."

"You already have."

The movie ended in a flash of white light, momentarily illuminating Zara's face. In that timeless instant, he read the genuine caring echoed in her words. She was so beautiful. So filled with compassionate warmth. No wonder Kadar protected her with such ferocity. She was a woman born to be treasured. Malik drew her close, gathering in her essence—her delicious scent, the musical cadence of her voice, the poetry of her movements. It all combined to make her the most unique woman he'd ever known.

Even more than that, she'd pleased him with her show of unquestioning trust. And though she hadn't taken it quite far enough, it was a start. He could only hope they'd have enough time for that start to reach completion.

Eventually Kadar would hear of the presence of "the Scourge" and learn that he was often alone with Zara.

When that happened, matters would fast come to a head. He needed tomorrow. Zara needed tomorrow, too. So much rested on her, more than she could possibly realize. If Kadar returned too soon, before she was ready for that confrontation, they both stood to lose everything. The bond that joined them wouldn't hold.

He forked his hands into her hair and smiled down at her. He'd just have to show her the trust she'd showed him, believe she'd follow her heart when that final test came. And until then...

"One kiss, Zara," he whispered. "Kiss me as you did when the stars were above us and the sand beneath and the world was ours alone. Kiss me as though we had forever to spend in each other's arms."

Tears glittered in her eyes like gold dust. "We don't have forever and we both know it. But I'll kiss you as though spending the rest of my life in your arms is what I want more than anything else in the world." She feathered her mouth across his. "Because it's the truth."

"Are you sure you're feeling all right, Rasha?" Zara asked in concern.

"I'm fine. It's just a pang. Now finish telling me about your latest gift from Malik. If it's anything like the first, I'm prepared to be delightfully shocked."

"Yes, it was like the first, only different. Yes, you'll be quite shocked. I certainly was. And no, it's not just a pang. You're in labor, aren't you?"

Rasha waved aside Zara's concern. "It will be a while before the baby comes. The girls took a full day before making an appearance." She squirmed to a more comfortable position. "Now tell me what happened at this driving-in theater. Did you really watch a movie or were you busy with more interesting activities?"

Before Zara could respond, a maid appeared in the doorway and Rasha made a face. "I assume she's here for you. No doubt Malik's waiting with his final gift. You should go before he becomes impatient."

"Learning patience will be good for him. I'm more concerned about you."

"There are plenty of people around to help me," Rasha said firmly. "There's nothing to worry about. It's not like I haven't given birth before."

Zara didn't argue, well aware she wouldn't win this particular battle of wills. Nevertheless, Hakem had asked that she keep him informed about Rasha's condition and she intended to do just that before joining Malik.

Tonight would bring his final gift. After that, Hakem would announce her fate. It wouldn't be marriage to Malik, no matter how much she might wish it. Kadar would have to agree for that to happen, and he never would. Nor had Malik asked her to marry him. He'd said he wanted her, and she didn't doubt the truth of his assertion. He'd claimed they belonged to each other. And he'd mentioned keeping her...for a time. But he'd made neither an offer nor a commitment.

After sending a message to Hakem to update him on Rasha's condition, Zara returned to her room to prepare for her evening with Malik. Once again, he'd specified what she should wear. "Something you won't mind getting dirty," he'd ordered. That didn't leave her much choice. She rarely wore slacks, since Kadar had extremely traditional views on "appropriate" attire for his only daughter. But perhaps, just this once she could get away with it.

One of the pairs of slacks Malik had purchased looked like a skirt at first glance, the broad-legged design of brushed cotton a safe choice for "getting dirty." She teamed it with a simple high-necked collarless shirt with a dropped shoulder line and wide bell-shaped sleeves. That only left her hair. She started to put it up and then hesitated. It was their last day together and she'd wear it the way Malik liked best. Grabbing a straw hat to protect her from the late-afternoon sun, she walked to the atrium.

Malik was waiting and smiled warmly at her appearance. "You look perfect."

"I'm glad you approve."

He chuckled at her ominous tone. "I assume Kadar wouldn't?"

"Not a chance."

"Then we'll have to make certain you enjoy your last day of freedom." He held out his hand. "Are you ready?"

She linked her fingers with his. "What have you planned?"

"A surprise."

"They've all been surprises."

"This one's a bit different."

"Good different?"

"I hope you'll think so." Instead of the car he'd used the night before, a Jeep awaited them. Climbing in, he tossed her a pair of sunglasses. "You might also want to tuck your hair into your hat so it doesn't get blown."

"I wear it up and you take it down," she grumbled. "I wear it down and you tell me to put it up."

"Leave it down if you want. I don't mind in the least."

He put the Jeep in gear and headed for the side gate

out of the palace. Instead of leading toward the capital city, it ran straight into the desert. Instantly the breeze picked up her hair and whipped it around her head. She fought to tame the tangled strands, hastily braiding her hair before shoving it beneath her hat.

"How far?" she shouted.

"About an hour."

An hour. She grinned. That meant they were going to Habah Oasis, the prize of the desert. She'd been there a few times as a child. If memory served, a large spring formed a swimming area surrounded by climbing rocks. Although she couldn't recall a sandy beach like the one she'd created in California, visitors often used the oasis as a picnic area.

Fifty minutes later she saw that she'd guessed right. The sun had begun to sink into the desert sands as they approached their destination. Torches on tall stakes were thrust into the ground in anticipation of nightfall, lining the area like soldiers standing for inspection. Several dozen cars were parked at the edge of the oasis and Zara fought to hide her disappointment. She'd hoped they'd have the place to themselves. But it would seem Malik had other plans.

Parking the car, he switched off the engine and turned toward her. "Let me have your hat and sunglasses."

Curious, but reluctant to demand an explanation, she handed them over. "Anything else?"

"Did you bring a comb?"

"I have a brush in my purse."

She dug through her handbag until she found it. To her surprise, he took it from her and released her braid—with more care than she'd ever shown—before sliding the brush through the tangled strands in cautious, even strokes. She'd never had a man attend to her personal grooming needs before. It proved as intimate as it was seductive.

She knew without a doubt that if she swayed closer, Malik would take her into his arms and kiss her, regardless of their audience. She closed her eyes, forcing herself to be sensible and remain still. She'd begun to hate "sensible." She also hated the constraints her sense of duty placed upon her. More than anything she wanted to tumble into Malik's arms and beg him to make love to her. But she couldn't. Not while Hakem controlled her future.

Finally the torture ended. Returning the brush to her purse, he dropped her hat on her head, setting it at a rakish angle. "You look perfect."

"What's going on, Malik?" she asked. "Why does it matter how I look?"

"You'll see."

He opened the Jeep door and walked with her across the rocky scrub that edged the oasis. Families had gathered, the atmosphere upbeat. The children played games while the wives tended the fires. The men gathered in small groups, drinking coffee and enjoying heated discussions. Delicious aromas filled the air, reminding Zara of the night she'd celebrated Malik's birthday.

"I tried to make it a barbecue," he said as she led her toward the spring. "They're very popular in the United States. People gather at a park and roast hamburgers and hot dogs on a grill. Then they play baseball and have races."

"Not camel races, I assume?"

He grinned. "No."

"And what's the purpose of a barbecue?"

"It's a gathering for families and communities, sometimes for company employees. It helps cement their relationships.''

Families. The word gave her a pang. ''It sounds wonderful.''

He squeezed her hand. ''It will be.''

By the time they reached the spring, they were alone again, all except for an elderly lady who sat with her feet in the water, a fishing pole in hand, and a straw hat covering her snow-white hair. ''I don't think I've ever seen a woman fish before,'' Zara whispered. ''Is there anything worth catching?''

''The spring was stocked at one time. I don't know if it's been fished out or not.''

''Doesn't she care?''

''Why don't you ask her.''

Zara couldn't explain what drew her. She simply followed her instincts and picked her way across the stones littering the ground until she reached the edge of the water. ''Have you caught anything?'' she asked.

The woman froze. ''I'm sorry,'' she said in English. ''I don't speak Rahman.''

''That's all right. I speak English.'' Zara settled on a rock nearby, aware of an odd tension emanating from the woman. How strange to find a foreigner—an American woman, no less—all alone in the middle of the desert. Somehow she doubted it was pure coincidence. ''I was just wondering if you'd gotten any nibbles.''

''Not yet, but I have hope.''

She reeled in the line and set the pole to one side. Then she turned and looked fully at Zara. From beneath a wide-brimmed straw hat, the fading sunlight caught in hazel eyes, illuminating a distinctive blend of green

and gold—a shade Zara saw every day in her own mir-
ror.

"Hello, Sarah," the woman said with a nervous
smile.

CHAPTER TEN

ZARA'S hands collapsed into fists and she struggled for control. It took three tries before she could get the words out. "I...I know you, don't I?"

"Yes, my dear. You do."

Her throat closed over, making it a fight to ask the questions she desperately wanted answered. "Are you... Are you my grandmother?"

"I was." The woman's mouth twisted and her expression grew infinitely sad. "Once upon a time. I'm your mother's mother. My name's Lottie."

Instantly Zara launched herself off the rock and pelted through the shallows to the old woman's side. She dropped to her knees heedless of the stones and damp. Slowly she reached out and cupped her grandmother's lined face, searching the features one by one.

"I have your eyes," she murmured tearfully. "I always wondered who I took after. I knew it wasn't Mother."

Lottie fingered a strand of reddish-gold hair. "And you have my hair color, too. At least, my hair color years and years ago."

"And your nose and chin." Zara laughed through her tears. "I've wanted to find you for so long."

"So have I. Oh, my darling, so have I."

Then Zara was in her grandmother's arms, enveloped in the maternal warmth of her hug. For years she'd dreamt of this moment, uncertain of what sort of welcome she'd receive if they were ever to meet, never knowing whether she'd even find this woman with whom she shared so much. If it hadn't been for Malik, their reunion might never have taken place.

Malik!

She glanced over her shoulder toward where he'd been standing. He was gone. The tears came faster. Did he have any idea how much this moment meant to her? The only thing that would have made it more perfect was if he'd been there to share it with her. If ever the scales between them had been askew, they were balanced this night.

Lottie followed Zara's gaze. "He's a fine man, your Mr. Haidar."

"Yes. Yes, he is."

"I'm pleased you were able to find someone so special. I...I worried."

"That I might be forced into an unwanted marriage?" Her grandmother nodded and Zara closed her eyes against the irony. They shared a similar fear, one which might very well come to pass. Not that she'd burden Lottie with that information. There were far more important matters to discuss. Deliberately she changed the subject. "Tell me about my family. I want to be told everything. Do I have aunts and uncles? And what about cousins? Do they know about me? Will they accept me?"

"Oh, my darling, they'll accept you with open arms, just as I have. Your mother and I made a terrible mistake, parting for foolish reasons. I would have given anything to heal the breach years ago."

Zara gave her grandmother's hands a gentle squeeze. "We'll heal it now."

Lottie scrambled for a tissue. "Bless you for that," she managed to say. As soon as she'd recovered her composure, she opened a huge carryall and removed a photo album. "I came prepared," she warned with a quick laugh.

The next hour passed in a heartbeat. It wasn't until it had become too dark to see clearly that Malik returned. He wasn't alone. Others came, bringing dinner and torches, before leaving the three to their privacy.

Dinner was a raucous affair. Zara discovered her grandmother possessed a lively sense of humor, one Malik thoroughly enjoyed provoking. And somehow during the course of their meal, Lottie managed to draw Malik out about his past, evoking stories from the days of his youth when Rahman had been his world and ruling a kingdom his destiny.

After dinner, Lottie taught Zara how to fish, while Malik offered pointers. Not that they caught anything. Finally, thoroughly soaked and exhausted, they picked their way back along the rocky shoreline. The torches were beginning to sputter and Zara realized with a pang that the evening would soon end. Malik had given her a gift beyond price—her grandmother. But it hurt unbearably to know that she wouldn't be held in his arms this night. That their final moments together would end with a look, instead of a touch.

"It's time for me to turn in," Lottie announced with regret. She cupped Malik's face in her hands and kissed his cheek. "Thank you for giving me back my granddaughter."

He returned her embrace. "My pleasure, Lottie. I appreciate your flying all this way on such short notice. I expect Hakem will invite you to the palace for an extended visit. I'll give him the name of your hotel so he'll know where to contact you."

"That would be lovely." She turned to Zara. "Come give your grandmother a hug, my darling."

Zara flew into her arms. "This day has meant so much to me."

"And to me, as well. He's a good man," she added in a whisper. "Don't lose him."

Tears filled Zara's eyes again and she covered them with a laugh. "It's not up to me."

"He hasn't asked, yet?" Lottie chuckled, pinching Zara's cheek. "Don't you worry about that. He will. Anyone with an ounce of brains can see how much he adores you."

There wasn't any point in explaining. It would only upset her grandmother. Giving Lottie a final squeeze, Zara released her. "I'll phone you tomorrow."

Malik glanced her way as he offered his arm to Lottie. "If you'll gather our belongings, I'll escort your grandmother to her driver. I have one last surprise for you before we head back to the palace."

By the time he'd returned, she'd bundled their trash and folded the blanket, restoring the site to its former pristine condition. A nervous hope took root. Perhaps this evening would end in his arms, after all.

Malik doused all but one of the torches. Then he held out his hand. "Come."

The families who'd been there earlier were all gone, just as the campers had silently retreated from the Californian lakeside the night of his birthday. He led her to the edge of the oasis where the desert sands encroached on the spring-fed vegetation and spread the blanket she carried. Holding the torch high, he waved it twice before dousing it in the sand. Darkness descended and he guided her onto the blanket.

"For this, we have to lie down," he instructed.

He cushioned her head on his shoulder, his arms tight around her. In the distance Zara heard a rolling boom and then a spray of colors lit the nighttime sky. "Fireworks." She stared in wonder. "You arranged for fireworks."

"It's my understanding that the best barbecues end this way, and I wanted you to have the best. These are for you."

She curled up against him, her hand on his chest, close to his heart. A reassuring calm filled her as she felt the steady beat reverberate beneath her fingertips. The display lasted a full twenty minutes, ending in an explosion of colors that filled the sky and signaled the end to her three days with Malik. As the last color faded, she shut her eyes.

"I don't want it to be over."

He smoothed the hair from her cheek. "We have no choice."

She acknowledged the truth with a quick nod, determined not to allow her emotions to ruin the beauty of the evening. She drew a shallow breath. "Thank you for finding my grandmother."

"Alice tracked her down. I merely visited her and arranged for her flight here."

"Still... I don't know how to explain how much I appreciate—" Her voice broke. She wouldn't cry. She wouldn't! "You've given me so much."

"It can never be as much as you've given me." He rolled toward her and levered onto an elbow, exploring her face with his fingertips. One by one, he traced her features, as though setting them to memory. He hesitated when he felt the dampness clinging to her lashes, before deliberately brushing away the tears. "You returned my past to me. You made me whole again. It was only right I try to do the same for you.''

''I just helped you remember the good times instead of the bad.''

''And in the process, you lost your opportunity to explore your roots and find your American family. I wanted to give back all you missed by being so generous.''

''Malik—''

He sealed the rush of words by sliding his thumb across her lips. ''There's one final question I want to ask before we leave.'' He splayed a hand across her belly, sending warmth cascading through her. ''Have you any idea whether or not you carry my child?''

''It's too soon to know for sure.'' She could only hope and pray that she did. She moistened her lips. ''You're going to leave Rahman, aren't you?''

''Hakem gave me three days. Tonight is the last of the three.''

''What will happen to you?'' *To us?*

''Don't think about it. Don't waste the last moments of our time together on what can't be changed.''

Despair filled her. ''Take me with you. Please, Malik.''

He shook his head. ''It won't solve anything. Kadar will simply come after you again. Besides, I promised Hakem I wouldn't.''

''And you're a man of honor,'' she said unevenly. ''A man who'd never go back on his word.''

''My word of honor is all I have.''

So simple. So absolute. And so integral to the man he was. ''Then I won't ask for what you can't give.''

''There is one thing I can offer.''

She smiled up at him. It was a tremulous smile, but

perhaps the dark concealed that fact from him. "I'll gladly accept whatever it is."

He lowered his head and kissed her. It was a kiss of such sweetness that the tears finally slipped free. This man completed her, aligned her, filled her heart and soul with a sense of rightness. Passion underscored the kiss, held carefully in check, and it was then that Zara fully understood how empty her life would become when Malik left.

She wrapped her arms around his neck, clinging, putting all of herself into that one kiss, determined to give him something to remember when they parted, just as desperate to give herself a final memory to treasure during the bleak days ahead.

Sudden lights exploded around them and at first Zara thought the fireworks had resumed. It wasn't until Malik rolled over and swept her protectively behind him that she realized that history was repeating itself. Kadar stood over them, his fury a terrifying force.

"Take your hands off my daughter!"

Malik slowly gained his feet. This moment had been coming for a full decade. It had been inevitable, brewing just beyond reach, building from a fitful storm to a mighty clash of the elements. The day had come for that storm to break. This wasn't just about Zara anymore, but about control and power and destiny. Years ago, Kadar had succeeded in bending him to his will. It wouldn't happen again.

"She's mine, Kadar," Malik stated with calm finality. "And this time you won't take her from me."

"Not only will I take her, I'll see that she marries Hakem. He's in my debt. He won't dare refuse my demands." He signaled to his sons. "Escort our stubborn prince to the palace. We finish this tonight, once and for all. Zara? Will you come on your own or must I carry you as I did before?''

She rose gracefully to her feet and lifted her chin. Malik smiled at the innate pride and hard-won serenity, amused that he found such personal satisfaction in an act for which he could neither take credit nor control. ''I come willingly,'' she announced. ''It's past time this matter was settled.''

For a brief moment, Kadar appeared disconcerted. Then he jerked his head toward the waiting vehicles. ''Take them.''

The king did not look pleased to see any of them. In fact, Hakem looked downright furious. ''Is it just me or is there something terribly ironic about an outraged father catching his daughter necking with her lover on a blanket beneath a full moon.''

''You dishonor my daughter!'' Kadar protested. ''She isn't his lover.''

''That's precisely what she is and no doubt what she'd like to be in the future, if the choice were hers.''

''But it isn't.''

Hakem ignored him, fixing his gaze on Malik. ''You wished to introduce Zara to American culture. I believe you've succeeded.''

''So it would seem,'' Malik said with a slight smile.

Kadar glared at the king in outrage. ''You knew about this? You encouraged his pursuit of my daughter.''

''Yes.''

''You've gone too far, Hakem. You owe me for supporting your rule, for not taking the throne when I had the chance.''

''The throne was never yours to take,'' Hakem retorted. ''You spent a fortune removing Malik and made yourselves countless enemies in the bargain. Had you attempted more back then, you'd have lost everything. So, let's have honesty between us. *That's* why you supported my rule.''

"Maybe so," Kadar conceded the point. "But while the years have passed, I haven't been sitting idle. I've had time to solidify my position. Defy me and I'll take the throne here and now."

It was the threat Malik had been waiting for. He fixed Kadar with an icy gaze and snapped his fingers. A servant darted forward, carrying an elaborately carved teak box. Flipping open the lid, Malik removed a dozen thick gold chains, each bearing a different amulet. He allowed them to stream through his fingers. "Your support is gone, Kadar."

The older man blanched, the breath hissing through his teeth. "What is this?"

"You know what it is. It's been put to a vote by the ruling families, just as it was ten years ago when you forced me from the throne. These amulets are the answer to your latest threat. The families have chosen who they'll support."

"No! They'd never support you over me—"

Malik tossed the amulets into the box and slammed the lid shut. The sound cracked through the room, bringing instant silence. "When last I confronted you, I was a boy. Now I'm a man, with a man's power. You won't take what's mine again. Hakem will not lose the throne to you, any more than I will lose Zara. You have failed, old man."

Kadar sliced his arm through the air. "You're an outcast! Those amulets mean nothing. The families won't support you now any more than they supported—"

"It's been decided," Hakem interrupted. "The vote

was cast and those amulets are a pledge of unconditional support for Haidar rule. I warn you, push this and you'll lose everything.''

"You forget something else, Kadar.'' Malik smiled coldly. "There's every chance that Zara carries my child. If she marries Hakem, her child—*my child*—would inherit the throne you seek so obsessively.''

"And if she marries Malik, I will see to it that their son will still inherit,'' Hakem added. "Wrong shall be made right. What you took from my cousin will be restored. I promise you that.''

"There might not be a child with Malik,'' Kadar began, his desperation beginning to show. "In which case her marriage to you—''

"She will never bear a child of mine,'' the king interrupted harshly. "For any marriage between us will go unconsummated.''

"Would you put your daughters on the throne?'' Kadar scoffed.

"That won't be necessary. If Malik has no children to inherit the throne, my son will accept the honor. The son Rasha delivered two short hours ago.'' Hakem allowed that to sink in before continuing more gently. "You can't win this one, old man. Would you lose your place of honor among us? Would you lose your daughter over your own stubborn foolishness? She wants Malik and he wants her. As for the throne... It was never yours to take and never will be. Give up this senseless pursuit.''

Kadar closed his eyes. "Is this true, Zara? You would take the Scourge?''

She stepped forward. "Without a moment's hesitation.''

Hakem held up his hand. "Not so fast. I have a great

deal of respect for my cousin. Too much to join him with just any woman. She must be worthy of the honor.''

Apprehension filled Zara. Worthy? How in the world could she prove herself worthy? "What must I do?''

"It's what you must say,'' Malik explained gently.

That was easy. She turned to face him. "I love you with all my heart and soul,'' she stated with utter sincerity.

He shook his head. "I'm sorry, my sweet. That's not good enough.''

"This is ridiculous,'' Kadar tried again.

"Silence!'' Hakem roared. "You may still get your wish. If I don't judge her worthy of Malik, I will take her as my wife, regardless of her wishes. It is my right as her king. You will be satisfied, old man. But you will find that satisfaction a bitter dish.''

"What more do you want?'' she whispered for Malik's ears alone.

He stepped back, folding his arms across his chest. "I can't help you, Zara. You must figure this part out for yourself.''

She closed her eyes in despair. What else could she say other than she loved him? What could be more important than that? What sort of words would convey her feelings for him? She adored him. He was the most honorable man she'd ever known. From the moment they'd met, she'd realized he was nothing like the man she'd been expecting, that all the stories she'd heard had been exaggerations and lies built on a foundation of—

Her eyes flew open. "I believe in you and trust you with my life.''

The warmth of his gaze was the most exhilarating

sight she'd ever witnessed. "And why is that, my love?"

"Because you're the most honest, honorable man I've ever met."

"I'm a murderer. I'm the Scourge of Rahman."

She shook her head. "No, Malik. You didn't kill Jeb."

"Because it was an accident?"

"No!" She understood now, and turned to face her stepfather. "He didn't kill Jeb. He wasn't the one behind the wheel. Nothing you say will ever convince me he was. Because if he'd been responsible, he'd have admitted it from the start. I don't know who ran down my brother, but it wasn't Malik."

With those words, she'd lifted the weight of a decade worth of pain and grief from Malik's soul. She'd brought his life full circle. In one act of blind faith, she'd restored his lost honor and made him whole. "Thank you, my heart," he murmured. Glancing at Hakem, he smiled. "A worthy bride, wouldn't you agree?"

The king inclined his head. "More than worthy. If I weren't so fortunate in my own choice, I'd envy you."

"There's no one else who could have killed Jeb," Kadar protested. "Malik had just had a fight with Asim. He'd threatened my family and left my home in anger. It was his car involved."

Malik stood firm. "It was my car that ran him down. But I wasn't the one behind the wheel."

Zara struggled to deal with the ramifications of that simple statement. "Someone else used your car?" The idea shocked her. At the time of the incident, Malik had been the heir to the throne. It would have been a brave soul—or a foolhardy one—who would joyride in a vehicle emblazoned with the palace seal.

"There's no other way the accident could have occurred." Malik thrust his hand through his hair. "I've gone over this in my mind again and again through the years. I did leave Kadar's angry and I did make threats. But they were political threats, not ones of physical violence."

Kadar swept that aside. "All right! So perhaps it was an accident instead of murder. That doesn't change the fact that you climbed behind the wheel of your Jeep and, in a fit of recklessness, stomped on the accelerator. If you'd been more careful, if you'd been going slower, you'd never have lost control and hit Jeb. And even after killing my stepson, you lied to protect your inheritance."

Malik shook his head. "You're wrong. By the time I got outside, the accident had already occurred. I tried to help Jeb." He turned to Zara, regret carving deep grooves alongside his mouth. "I'm sorry, my heart. There was nothing to be done but comfort your brother until he died. If it helps any, he wasn't alone at the end."

"It was not Malik," Hakem said to Kadar, his voice edged with impatience. "Look elsewhere for your murderer."

Kadar's hands folded into fists. "Who?"

Malik released his breath in a sigh of regret. "You know who. You just can't bring yourself to admit the truth."

"*No!* It was *not* one of my sons!"

Silence reigned at the telling denial.

And then Paz stepped forward, his face white, his

hands trembling. "Yes, Father. It was. I was the one who killed Jeb."

"No." Despair and desperation haunted Kadar's gaze. "No. You were but a child."

"A child tempted by an available car. I had seen all my older brothers drive, watched friends of a similar age climb into the driver's seat. I thought I should be allowed, too. Jeb warned me not to, but I didn't listen." Pain raged in his voice. "My foot slipped and I couldn't stop. The car careened off the pavement and hit Jeb. I panicked. And I ran."

"But you were forbidden to touch a car," Kadar protested feebly. "You were too young."

Paz laughed without humor. "Why should that matter? I was the son of Kadar. Rules didn't apply to me."

"Why didn't you tell us this long ago?" Zara demanded, hurt beyond measure. "Why did you allow Malik to take the blame?"

"You know why. Father was so angry and I was afraid. I thought if I were to admit what I'd done—" He confronted Kadar. "I…I'm not sure what I thought you'd do. Disown me. Or make me leave the country, like you did Malik. If you were capable of bringing down a king, what would you do to a mere son?"

"Ah, Paz." Kadar's voice broke. "You were an eleven-year-old child. Did you think so little of me, of your own honor—"

Hakem broke in. "Perhaps if you'd paid more attention to your children than your political ambitions, he'd have had the fortitude to come to you. Perhaps if he'd seen you put honor and integrity above vengeance, he'd have learned right from wrong. This will not sit well with the ruling families, Kadar. I suggest you consider how best to make amends."

For an endless moment Kadar fought an inner battle. At long last, he took a deep breath and turned to face Malik. "I can start by offering my humble apologies. I'm sorry, Prince Haidar. I was blinded by my own ambitions."

"No doubt my wife will school me in the fine art of forgiveness," Malik retorted. "Though I suspect it will take time for me to fully grasp the concept."

"She will make you a fine wife." Kadar bowed low, a formal, submissive gesture. "May she bless you with many sons."

"Have we settled this matter?" Hakem asked. "I have a wife and child who require my attention."

Kadar inclined his head. "It's not settled and I doubt it will be for some time to come. But it can wait until a more appropriate occasion when tempers have cooled and forgiveness isn't such a remote possibility." Signaling to his sons, he retired from the room with surprising dignity.

"I assume you can take things from here?" Hakem asked Malik.

"Count on it."

"In that case, I'll give Rasha the good news. I think she's been more anxious about this than the birth of our own child."

And then they were alone. "So what now?" Zara asked unsteadily.

"What do you mean?"

"I mean now that you've won, what do you plan to do with me?"

Tenderness gleamed in Malik's eyes. "Don't you know?"

"I know what's been said here today. But you've never mentioned your plans to me."

"Never...?" His brows drew together. "What are you talking about?"

"You've said you want me. You've made love to me. You've claimed me as your own." She twisted her hands together, wishing for the serenity she'd achieved on other stressful occasions. For some reason, it had deserted her. "But you've never said the words."

"Of course I—" He froze, his frown deepening. "I haven't, have I?"

She shook her head. "I need you to tell me how you feel, Malik, the same as you needed to hear the words earlier."

Tenderly he gathered her hands in his. "I, my sweet, am a fool."

"That may be, but those aren't quite the words I was hoping to hear."

"Don't you know?" He kissed her fingers one by one. "Within these hands rests my heart." He leaned forward and sealed her lips with his. "And behind these lips..."

"My opinion is yours?" she asked hopefully.

Laughter broke from him, light and free and natural. "Let's not get carried away." Gathering her close, he kissed her again. It was a kiss marked with desperation, an embrace that acknowledged how close they'd come to losing everything. It wasn't until a soft moan of longing slipped through the air that his tension eased. Slowly he pulled back. "You give me life, Zara. You complete me. And I love you more than any mere words can state."

"As I love you," she whispered.

"The past is finally behind us." His hand slipped downward, settling low on her abdomen. "Here lies our future."

"You don't know that for sure," she protested in a shaken voice.

"Yes, I do. Our child will be a son, born in the spring at a campsite near a mountain-fed lake. He'll come into this world beneath a benevolent moon, with a sky full of dazzling stars blessing his birth. The wind will sing to him and the fire warm him, while the gentle wash of water lapping against the sand will soothe his passage from one world to the next." He gathered her close. "He will be a child of grace. He will be a king who will reign with truth and honor and compassion. And he'll watch his parents grow old, secure in their love for him and for each other and for his many brothers and sisters. It will be a good life, Zara. I promise you that."

"With you beside me, how can it be anything else?"

"Since I've neglected to ask you before, I'll ask now. Will you marry me?"

She cupped his face in her palms. "How can I refuse? My king has commanded it."

He lifted an eyebrow. "And when your king commands, you obey?"

She grinned, lifting onto tiptoes to feather her mouth across his. "If nothing else, I give it serious consideration."

And then there was no more discussion, no need for further conversation. The future was set. It only needed time to bring it to full fruition.

Harlequin Romance®

Experience the ultimate desert fantasy with this thrilling new Sheikh miniseries!

Four best-loved Harlequin Romance® authors bring you strong, proud Arabian men, exotic eastern settings and plenty of tender passion under the hot desert sun....

Look out for:

His Desert Rose by Liz Fielding
(#3618) in August 2000

To Marry a Sheikh by Day Leclaire
(#3623) in October 2000

The Sheikh's Bride by Sophie Weston
(#3630) in November 2000

The Sheikh's Reward by Lucy Gordon
(#3634) in December 2000

Available in August, September, October and November wherever Harlequin Books are sold.